# MARY CRAWFORD

# Finding Hope

## HIDDEN HEARTS
## Protection Unit Book 4

# Copyright

# HIDDEN BEAUTY SERIES

Until the Stars Fall from the Sky
So the Heart Can Dance
Joy and Tiers
Love Naturally
Love Seasoned
Love Claimed
If You Knew Me (and other silent musings) (novella)
Jude's Song
The Price of Freedom (novella)
Paths Not Taken
Dreams Change (novella)
Heart Wish
Tempting Fate
The Letter
The Power of Will

# HIDDEN HEARTS SERIES

Identity of the Heart
Sheltered Hearts
Hearts of Jade
Port in the Storm (novella)
Love is More Than Skin Deep
Tough
Rectify
Pieces (a crossover novel)
Hearts Set Free
Freedom (a crossover novel)
The Long Road to Love (novella)

HIDDEN HEARTS - PROTECTION UNIT
Love and Injustice
Out of Thin Air
Soul Scars

OTHER WORKS:
The Power of Dictation
An Everyday Guide to Scrivener 3 for Mac
An Everyday Guide to Scrivener 3 for Windows

# DEDICATION

To those who nurture
love
in the middle of
pain and chaos
and find a way
to help others.

You make the world
a better place.

# Chapter One

# Dakota

A wad of paper bounces off the back of my head. It causes me to utter a cuss word under my breath as I try to still my racing heart. I spin my office chair around and glare at my coworker.

"Need something, Jamie?"

"You've been staring at that same screen for twenty minutes. I figured you were stuck."

"I'm not stuck. I'm second-guessing myself."

"What do you mean? I thought you found a positive match?"

"I did. It's just that the demographics of this guy don't really scream child killer, you know what I mean?"

"You of all people should know how a family looks on paper doesn't really mean squat."

"Yeah, I know. I hate this part. Knowing half the truth is sometimes more painful than knowing nothing. I'm about to drop a truth bomb on some unsuspecting family who has the unfortunate luck to be related to a murdered child."

"You never know. Your call could help provide more closure than they've had in years. Are you gonna call directly or go through the local LEO?"

"I think I'll use the local law enforcement agency. I want to cushion the blow. Quite frankly, I don't want to be the bad guy because I'm not sure Nicholas Weston is the final target. I may need his cooperation to build the case against the real killer."

"Where did you say Weston lives? Orlando?"

I flip through the file in front of me. "Nope, he's in Gainesville."

"Wow! It is your lucky day. I met Detective Cody Erickson at a law enforcement conference a couple years ago. He has a passion for cases involving kids. He would be perfect for you."

I tuck my hair behind my ear and wrinkle my nose. "Are you matchmaking again, Jamie? You know how I hate that."

"Okay, I know I have a tarnished reputation, but I swear I'm not playing Cupid. As far as I know Cody is married to the district attorney. I figured you would enjoy working with him just because he is an excellent cop."

"Sorry, I shouldn't jump to conclusions —"

Jamie snorts. "Yeah … about that. I apologize for setting you up with that equipment salesman. I totally wasn't aware he had a wife and kids in Minnesota."

I grin. "Umm-hmm, that wasn't your finest hour. But I learned way more about ice fishing than I ever wanted to know. Anyway, do you have any contact information for this Detective Erickson?"

"I'll text it to you. By the way, this is a temporary truce

in my matchmaking mission. You deserve to be with someone great. I don't know why you have a tough time. You look like a model. You are a beautiful blonde with legs a mile and a half long."

I roll my eyes. "You know there's more to my story than that." Impulsively, I stick my tongue out at Jamie. "I'm just fine with my books and Mr. Pawsome. We don't need anyone else."

Jamie clicks his tongue at me. "I'm telling you, Dakota. You are at extreme risk for becoming a sad, pathetic stereotype."

I hold my hands up in front of me in a motion of surrender. "Tell me something I don't know. Besides, I only have one cat. I'm pretty sure to be considered a deranged cat lady I'd have to have a whole colony."

Jamie chuckles. "The fact that you know the scientific term for a group of cats speaks volumes."

"Well … Yeah. Us science-y types tend to know all the big words."

I stare at the text message with my finger hovering over the keyboard before I sigh and pick up the phone. Either way I approach this, it's likely to be confusing.

"This is Detective Erickson, may I help you?" he answers.

I clear my throat. I am far more comfortable with scientific data than I am with people. "Hello, this is Dr. Dakota Crenshaw. I'm calling from Fitzgerald Forensics."

"The DNA Sleuths?"

I breathe a sigh of relief. If he knows who we are, this might be an easier conversation than I expected. "That's us. I called to see if you are interested in questioning a potential DNA match for me."

"Sounds ominous. What kind of match?"

Even though Detective Erickson can't see me, I cringe at his question. "We have a potential DNA match to a Baby Jane Doe."

"From here?" he asks incredulously. "As far as I know, we don't have any missing infants."

"No, the missing child isn't from Gainesville. She was found in Owl Creek, Tennessee."

"I see. So, what is the connection to Florida?"

"We have reason to believe there is a partial DNA match to the child living in your community. I would like you to ask him a few questions for me. I need to confirm we have the right person."

"Understood. How can I help?"

"My research suggests baby Jane Doe is a close relative of Nicholas Weston. I believe he resides in your county."

I hear Detective Erickson blow out a breath as if he's been punched. "Nick Weston? Are you sure?"

"Statistically, I'm more than satisfied. Why?"

"Nick is one of the good guys. He helped rescue my former partner from a stalker. I can't imagine he would be mixed up with something like this."

"With all due respect, Detective Erickson, our world is full of people who no one believes are capable of horrible acts, yet they still happen."

"Point taken. Still, I think you're barking up the wrong

tree. Nick is one of the most principled people I know."

"I hope you're right. But DNA appears to tie him to a murdered child."

"Do you want me to step aside and assign this questioning to another coworker since I know Nick?"

"Whatever you feel comfortable with. I just want to figure out who Baby Jane Doe is."

"Do you want to be present for the interrogation?"

"I wish! Unfortunately, I don't have a travel budget, and Virginia is a bit of a commute from Gainesville."

"I serve as a consultant on the Cold Case Squadron. Since you are working on the case of a missing child, I'll get you covered."

I draw in a deep breath. "This case tugs on my heartstrings. I'd love to find some answers. But I am more of a behind-the-scenes kind of person."

"Perfect, if I were you I would follow your instincts. At this point, you have the best grasp of the evidence. Your presence would be helpful."

"I have to testify in court tomorrow and possibly the next day. When I finish, I guess I am headed to Florida. I hope my visit resolves more questions than it creates."

"Great! I look forward to working with you. Let's give that little girl an identity."

# CHAPTER TWO

# NICK

The sound of the noisy bar is almost enough to quiet my thoughts. Absently, I study the crack in the stained glass partition behind the bartender. My mother would love to get her hands on the intricately patterned glass. She loves to reclaim old art like this.

"Nick Weston! I never thought I'd see this in a million years!" I whirl around to face my former boss, Logan Anthony.

"See what?" I blurt, as I try to process his presence. Last I knew, Logan was still head of security for Aiden O'Brien in Oregon.

Logan points to my glass. "I never figured you'd return to the 'scene of the crime'. I really didn't expect you to be drinking Jack Daniels."

"What would Katie think if she knew you refer to the place you met as the 'scene of the crime'?"

"My wife would fall off her chair laughing. She's the one who came up with the moniker."

"I should've guessed. By the way, this is plain old iced tea. I'll leave the JD for Katie's consumption. What are you doing here? Florida is a long way from your neck of the woods."

"Tara tore her Achilles tendon and needs to have surgery. Aidan postponed the tour and gave us some time off. When we get back to work, we'll have to double up on bookings. It worked out well though. Can you believe my niece, Ketki, is getting ready to graduate from high school? Katie has been out running errands with her brother. She should be here in a few."

"Wow! Time sure flies. It seems like I'm not the only one visiting ghosts from the past."

"Nah, we thought it would be fun to go dancing for a change. These days, most of our 'dates' include chicken nuggets and French fries. My parents offered to babysit Kaden and we fully intend to take them up on the offer."

It's all I can do not to roll my eyes. "Gee, it's terrible your life is full of domestic bliss."

"It is great. I'm thankful for Katie's botched wedding every single day. I don't know what my life would be like without her. How about you? Last I heard you were headed home for a visit."

I pause to take a drink. For the first time in more than fifteen years, I find myself wishing my iced tea was really Jack Daniels. I shudder at the thought. When I was still a teenager, my father died of alcohol poisoning. If anyone knows that alcohol creates far more problems than it solves, it's me.

"Let's just say I don't see my future filled with domestic bliss. Not everyone is as lucky as you."

"That's rough. I take it things didn't work out with Cheryl?"

A bitter taste rises from my throat. "I'd say they

worked out just fine for her. For me? Not so much."

"What do you mean?"

"I went home with high hopes that we could patch things up one last time. I figured since she asked me to help get her grandmother's affairs settled after Helen passed away, she must be interested in working things out. Man, oh man, things were a mess too. Helen had dementia and left tons of unpaid bills behind. Since Cheryl and I were finally working together for a change, I thought there might be a future between us."

"Reasonable assumption," Logan shells a peanut and pops it in his mouth.

"I thought so too. But I couldn't have been more wrong. As many times as Cheryl and I have been off and on, I never expected her to pick another guy. Our timing has always been rotten. First, she hated all my deployments. Now, I missed out because I'm on the road so much with Identity Bank."

"Yeah, our travel schedule can be tough on relationships. Sometimes, even Tara and Aidan have issues."

"Exactly! I thought Cheryl and I could work through our issues if we just had a chance to talk. I must be naïve … or gullible … or just plain stupid, but I thought we had a chance — right up until I watched her walk down the aisle with somebody else."

"That sucks. No one deserves that kind of pain. I gotta ask, why did you go to her wedding?"

"That's a good question. Family loyalty, I guess. My grandma was close friends with Cheryl's grandmother. My Maw-maw would've been really disappointed if I didn't take her to the wedding. Cheryl was like her goddaughter."

Logan winces. "Family expectations are tough. Couldn't your brother step up for a change?"

I scrub my hand down my face. "I'm not sure what happened. Milo is on the outs with everyone again. So, I just swallowed my pride and went to make my grandma happy."

"I'm not just saying this because we're friends. I don't know who Cheryl married, but she missed out on a standup guy —"

I put my hands up in a gesture of timeout. "Don't you do it!"

"Do what?" Logan asks with an expression of studied innocence.

"I don't need another lecture about how there are plenty of women in the sea and I just have to wait for the right one to come along. My life isn't some twisted fishing expedition."

Logan leans back in his chair. "I hear you. It sucks when everyone else around you is happily in love and it seems like it will never happen to you. I was in your shoes once. I'm not going to give you the tired old line that you can just find someone else. I just want you to be open to the idea." He gestures around the quaint bar, just a few steps above a dive bar. "As you know, I never expected to find the love of my life in a place like this, but it happened."

"Yeah, that's great for you. But I don't seem to have your kind of luck."

"I'm sorry. Are you going to stick around? I'm sure Katie would love to see you."

I grimace. "Normally, I'd say yes — but I'm terrible company today."

Logan gives me a little salute. "Understood. Take care of yourself. If you change your mind, we'll be around for a while."

I hit the contacts button on my phone. "Anything change?"

"Nope. Katie and I are ridiculously predictable in our old age."

"News flash, Boss. You always were. I'll try to get my head on straight and give you guys a call before you go back to Oregon."

"If you want a change of pace, you could always come back to work for Silent Beats. We miss you."

"Nothing personal, but the last thing I need right now is an endless supply of love songs."

Logan chuckles. "Love songs are good for your soul."

I stare at my drink as I swirl the tea around in my cup. "Maybe for some people, but for me those songs are a reminder of what I don't have."

When my phone rings, I throw the remote control on the couch. Heck, it's not like I was paying attention anyway.

I answer it, expecting it to be Tristan with details of my new assignment. I'm surprised when I hear a female voice instead.

"Whatever you're selling, I am not in the mood to buy. I don't need to go on a cruise or buy a time-share and no one is going to arrest me for suspicious activity involving my Social Security number."

A light laugh bubbles up from the person on the other

end of the phone. "I should hope not!"

"Not to be rude or anything, but who is this?" I demand as I rub the persistent throbbing in my temple.

"Stupid allergies! No one recognizes my voice because I sound like a frog. This is Mindy."

"Wow! They must be hitting you hard. I had no idea it was you. Congrats on your newest single. It's moving right up the charts."

"Thanks. That one is pretty special to us. Elijah is playing backup guitar on it. I consider it a tribute to our love story."

"That's cool. I am thrilled you guys are doing so well. I haven't heard from you in a while — let me guess, Aidan is planning some huge shindig and you are responsible for rounding everyone up?"

"I wish. That would be fun. But that's not why I called."

"It's not? What's up?"

Mindy heaves a deep sigh. "You know about my gift, right?"

"Of course I do. You saved Katie and Elijah's dad. I know enough about the way you and Tara work to get that you haven't called to tell me I'm going to win the lottery." I swallow hard before I mutter, "How bad is it?"

"Bad enough for me to call you. I don't have a lot of detail. It's all very confusing. But you need to look at your past — no matter how painful. It's a matter of life and death."

"Oh trust me, I've been examining my past a little too closely these days. At the moment all I feel is pain and regret."

"Just remember love is stronger than pain. I wish I had more answers for you, but please don't lose hope."

I sigh. "It may be a little too late for that advice. Honestly, this month has been a rough one."

"I understand. Just keep an open mind and answer your phone. Don't forget that you can save some people, but not others. Please pay attention, my warning is important."

With that, my phone goes dead. Mindy's words make the hair on the back of my neck stand up. Her precognition skills are legendary and I have a hunch my life is about to get worse before it gets better.

I practically jump out of my skin when my phone vibrates in my hand. "Hello?" I answer, cringing at the breathless quality.

"Hey, Nick. Did I call you at a bad time?"

"Cody? Nah, I was just talking to Mindy and watching TV."

"If you have a moment, would you mind coming down to the station. Detective Lawrence would like to ask you a few questions."

"Pauline? Why would Pauline need to ask me questions? Didn't I tell you guys the alleged break-in at the Voigt's turned out to be their teenager trying to cover for being out past curfew?"

"Good to know, but that's not what this is about. It would be easier for Pauline to discuss the matter with you in person."

"Can't you just ask me whatever you need to over the phone? You know me, I'm an open book."

Cody sighs. "I wish I could, but I need to play this one

by the book."

My stomach lurches. The fact that Cody is using his formal detective voice is enough to make my heart race.

"Fair enough. I'm on my way."

# CHAPTER THREE

# DAKOTA

I watch as a dark-haired detective flits around the room. She reminds me of the teenager who comes to walk my mother's dogs. Her eyes are full of mirth as she hands me a cup of coffee. "You may want to try a small sip first. Detective Palmer tells me it's rude for me to make the coffee as thick as road tar. I still don't have the knack of this new machine yet."

"It's all right. I can drink anything as long as it's hot and caffeinated."

"Hi, I'm Detective Lawrence, but you can call me Pauline. Detective Erickson thought he should keep his distance from this investigation since he and Nick Weston are friends. I mean, I've met him too. But we're not close buddies or anything."

"I'm Dr. Dakota Crenshaw. You can call me Dakota. I work for Fitzgerald Forensics as a forensic genealogist."

Pauline's eyes widen. "What kind of doctor are you?"

I blush. "This will show my ultimate nerdiness. I have a doctorate degree in statistics and I minored in history at Stanford."

"Okay, that's amaze-balls! I wish I was book smart."

"Obviously, you're not so shabby yourself, Detective. If you don't mind me asking, how old are you?"

Pauline winks at me. "Old enough to know better than to answer that question. My dad says my smarts are all dedicated to being a smarty-pants."

I hold my coffee cup up in salute. "Here's to smart women. May we figure out who this precious baby is."

Pauline grins. "That's the goal! Do you want to be the bad guy or the good guy?"

"I don't know," I stammer. "I'm usually a 'just the facts, ma'am' kind of gal."

"Good! We'll play it by ear. That's my favorite kind of interrogation."

My skepticism must be written all over my face. She pats me on the shoulder before she sits down. "Don't worry, I am great at this and have far more experience than it seems."

"I'm glad you do. I don't usually participate in this part of the case. I'm the person who puts the puzzle pieces together behind the scene."

"It'll be great for you to see the other side of a case for a change. It must be frustrating to put all the pieces together and then hand it off to someone else."

I shrug. "I never thought of it that way, but I suppose you're right. Sometimes, I testify about my DNA findings, but I don't usually get to see what you guys do."

"Well, let's get this show on the road." Pauline pushes a buzzer under the table. "Todd, can you escort Mr. Weston into interrogation room four?"

As Nick Weston strides confidently into the interrogation room, it becomes apparent the man is much more than a collection of genomes. As a scientist, I'm usually downright objective about life forms. But this particular life form is drop dead gorgeous. I'm not exactly sure what I expected Nick to look like, but this isn't it.

Pauline stands up to shake his hand. "Thanks for coming down, Nick. We really appreciate it."

"It's not a problem. But does anyone want to tell me why I'm not just shooting the breeze with Cody?"

"I'll get to that in a moment," Pauline gestures toward me. "Nick Weston, I'd like to introduce you to Dr. Dakota Crenshaw from Fitzgerald Forensics."

Nick's brow furrows as he pauses mid-handshake. "The DNA Sleuth Squad?"

I complete the handshake. "I'm impressed. Not many people are familiar with what we do."

Nick walks over to the empty chair and sits down. He crosses his ankle over his knee. "I'm a crime show junkie. A while back, I saw your boss solve a crime using DNA. He is quite the character. I've never seen anybody so passionate about their job."

I grin. "No doubt. Niles Fitzgerald loves what he does. His enthusiasm is contagious."

"That's great. What does all this have to do with me?" he asks.

"Since you profess a love of crime shows, you are probably familiar with DNA, correct?"

Nick studies me carefully. "Of course. I think most people are."

"So, Fitzgerald Forensics takes things a step further. We use familial DNA to try to solve cases. It's a combination of genealogy and biological science."

Nick blinks in surprise. "Are you saying my DNA was found at a crime scene?"

I shake my head. "Bluntly, I don't know. The DNA of our victim was somewhat degraded. I'd like to compare it to a pristine sample of yours."

Much to my surprise, Nick's face hardens and his eyes light with a flash of anger. He scrubs his hand through his short curly black hair. "This is bogus! My DNA isn't at any crime scene. This is because I'm black, right? Whatever you found, it's not from me. The last time I committed a crime, I was four years old."

At my skeptical look, he explains, "When I was a kid, I took the charity jar off the counter at the grocery store. I figured if no one else was using it, I might as well buy some candy."

I smirk. "My criminal history includes stealing from the offering plate at church. So, no judging here."

"I'm telling you, Cheryl must've put you up to this. I haven't done anything."

"Who is Cheryl?" Pauline and I ask in unison.

"Cheryl is my ex. I was planning to marry her right up until the time she married someone else. Needless to say, our last interaction was a tad contentious."

I cringe at the pain in his voice. Shuffling through the file in front of me, I look at it briefly. "No, there is no record here of any interaction with anyone named Cheryl.

The link to you was established purely through genetics. It's not a racial thing, I promise. You're a suspect based purely on science."

Nick slumps down in his chair and rests his head against the wall for a moment. "I'm sorry to sound so defensive, but I don't understand what's happening here. Maybe you should start from the beginning."

I take a computer-generated picture from the file and hand it to him. "Two years ago, this little girl was found stuffed in a well in Owl Creek, Tennessee. No one knows who she is or how she died."

Reluctantly, Nick takes the picture from me and studies it. "So, is this photograph based on predictive genome technology?"

"That … and her skeletal remains. We believe she was anywhere between eighteen months and two years old when she was killed. We don't know exactly how long she has been dead — except that her remains were skeletonized."

"She certainly looks like she could be related to my family." Nick's expression is somber as he murmurs, "Oh, you poor angel baby. Who would do something like this to you?"

Pauline clears her throat. "I'm sorry to have to ask this, Nick. Do you have any children?"

Nick's eyes widen in surprise. "Me? No!"

"Are you sure? Accidents sometimes happen," Pauline presses.

He shakes his head vehemently. "Not to me!" I raise an eyebrow.

He scrubs his hand down his face. "Look, I know it

sounds stupid. But my mom got pregnant as a teenager and married my dad. It didn't go well. So, I'm extraordinarily careful not to repeat history."

I don't know how Detective Lawrence feels about this interview, but I believe Nick is telling me the truth. "Take another look. Does the girl look familiar to you at all? Based on her DNA, I'd say she's related to you."

Nick's hands tremble as he holds the picture. He examines it carefully before placing it on the desk upside down. "I'm sorry. I honestly don't know who she is. I wish I did. No one deserves to die without a name."

"I agree. That's why I have been working so hard to find a DNA match."

"Speaking of DNA, how did you guys get mine? I don't think I've ever taken a test."

I leaf through the file and squint when I see the number. "I'm not sure exactly when you took your DNA test, but it looks like it was uploaded to the database about ten years ago."

A look of resignation crosses Nick's face. "Oh, that explains it. I remember now. I had to submit a DNA sample as part of my basic training."

When he catches me nodding, he asserts, "I know you don't believe me, but I don't know who this beautiful child is. If I did, I would tell you. Despite the DNA match, I think you have the wrong person."

"With your permission, I want to take another sample to make sure the database is correct. There is one more possibility. Do you have siblings or cousins?"

Nick winces. "I don't have any cousins because the whole family was wiped out in Hurricane Katrina right before I graduated from high school."

"I'm sorry. That's awful."

"It was. It devastated my mom. I have a brother, but we are not close."

Pauline taps her pen on a legal pad. "Any particular reason for that?"

Nick sighs. "No reason really. We're as different as oil and water. But Milo doesn't have any kids. Can DNA be wrong? Where do we go from here?"

"First, I get some spit from you to see if I can rule you out or definitively rule you in. Then, I'll do what I always do —"

The corner of Nick's mouth hitches up. "What's that?"

I level an even gaze at him. "I keep digging until I have answers."

"Fair enough," Nick concedes. "You want some help finding out who this angel baby is?"

His question brings me up short. "It depends on what kind of help. Sometimes, outside assistance is not all that helpful."

Nick glances over at Pauline. "If I can swing it, this would be the best possible kind of help. Professional, dedicated assistance."

I glance at Pauline with a questioning gaze. She shrugs. "If Nick can bring the Cold Case Squadron in, they are the best. Of course, I might be biased since my fiancé, Toby, is part of the team."

I reach out to shake Nick's hand. "This is the second time I've heard the Cold Case Squadron mentioned in glowing terms. If that's the caliber of help you are offering, I'll take it. This little girl haunts my dreams. I want her to find her way home."

# CHAPTER FOUR

# NICK

As I head down the hall toward my office, Ketki nearly mows me down with a hover board. I reach out to steady her. "Woah! Where's the fire?" It's then I notice the blond puff ball peeking around her. I squat down to pet the curious puppy. "Who's this?"

Ketki scoops up the puppy and cradles it to her chest. "This is Lady Gogo. Isn't she cool? Tuffy is getting old. His arthritis hurts him, even though he's taking medicine. So, Mitch told me I could start raising a puppy. If she's well behaved, Mitch is going to train her to be my stepdad's new seeing-eye dog."

"Clever name. This little fluff will have to grow a lot before she can be a service dog."

"I know. Mitch says she'll be the perfect size for John. He says Samoyed Golden Retriever crosses are super smart." She nudges the hover board with her foot. "I think he's right. Lady Gogo isn't even bothered by the hover board. I wanted to try her out with a wheelchair, but this is the closest thing I have."

"That's awesome. Are you excited for your

graduation?"

Ketki's fingers drum against the puppy's fur. "Yes … and no."

"I suppose you're going to miss your friends," I suggest.

Ketki tilts her head and looks right past me. "Nah, that's not it exactly. I don't really have very many friends except for Tristan's gaming team. But, I'm used to it. I'm not excited because I don't know where I'm going to go for college. My dad says my options are wide open and I can go to school anywhere I'd like."

"That sounds like a wonderful problem to have."

"Yeah, I know, right? Most of the kids in my school would kill to be in my shoes."

"So, what's the problem?"

"I'm good at too many things," Ketki states bluntly.

At my look of surprise, she clarifies. "I'm not bragging. I can't figure out what I want to do. I have so many interests I don't know what path to follow. You know when I was younger, I helped the police bust up a human trafficking ring? I loved using my computer skills to fight crime."

"Yeah, I heard about that. You did an amazing job."

"Thank you," she says as she blinks. "Some days, I think that's what I want to do. But then I think about Shelby. She's a really awesome teacher. She doesn't look down on people like me. There should be more teachers like that. Maybe I should become a teacher."

"I'm going to tell you something I wish my mom would've told me when I was graduating from high school."

"Don't drive so fast?" Ketki deadpans, referring to my well-known penchant for receiving speeding tickets.

Her delivery is so dry that her joke catches me off guard. I laugh out loud. "Okay, fair enough. My mom did say that. But I wish she would've let me know that I didn't have to have my life sorted out when I turned eighteen. It's a good thing too. Because nothing in my life has turned out the way I planned."

"You didn't plan to work for Tristan?"

"No, if you would have asked me what I planned to do after high school, I would've told you I was going to marry the prom queen and become a famous basketball player like LeBron James."

"I didn't even know you played basketball. You're not married, right?"

"No, I'm not. The girl I fell in love with just married someone else because she didn't love me as much as I loved her. I don't play basketball anymore because when I was in the military someone shot down my helicopter and I injured my hip."

"That sucks. What do you plan to do now?"

"Good question. Since I left Silent Beats, Tristan has been trying out other positions to see if he can find a good match for me."

"You didn't like it at Silent Beats? I love Mindy Whitaker's music. If I could sing, I'd want to be just like her."

"Mindy is the essence of cool. It's hard to explain, but I asked to be reassigned so that I could spend more time at home. I was hoping my girlfriend would approve of my job if I didn't travel so much."

"The same girlfriend who just married someone else?" Ketki asks incredulously.

I nod. "It may not have been my brightest career move. Anyway, like I said you don't have to know the whole plan in advance. Your plans will probably change anyway."

"That's what Shelby says. She told me to take a gap year and explore my options. That's why graduating makes me sad. My classmates are going away to college and I'll be stuck at home."

My cell phone rings. "I need to take this. If you ever need a sounding board, you know where to find me." As I grab my phone, it stops ringing in my hand.

"Don't forget my graduation party on Friday. My dad rented out the pizza parlor and arcade. If you don't come, I'm going to look stupid. Once, my dad planned a whole elaborate party for me and not a soul showed up. He was more disappointed than I was. I don't want that to happen again."

I rub my belly and grin. "If I can possibly make it, I'll be there. You know me, I love pizza. It should be the fifth food group."

"You're so silly. Made properly, pizza is a combination of all the food groups. Make sure you bring a friend or two to my party. My dad made it so that the games don't cost anything to play."

"Sounds good." My phone rings again. I wave at Ketki. "I need to get this. I'll see you and Lady Gogo another time."

I duck back into my office and answer my phone. "Go for Nick."

"Mr. Weston? This is Dakota Crenshaw. Did I call at a bad time?"

"No, this is perfect. I was just giving a few friendly words of advice to my friend who is graduating from high school."

Even on the phone, her laughter makes me smile. "Oh good gravy! High school seems so long ago. I still can't believe my fifteenth reunion is coming up next year. I hope you told her just to breathe and be herself."

"I told her something similar. My fifteenth reunion is also coming right up. I am planning to skip it."

"Why in the world would you do that? You're probably one of the hottest guys in your class." She pauses for a moment. I hear a soft groan. "Disregard what I just said. Apparently, I left my professional britches at home. I can't believe I just said that out loud. Maybe they shouldn't let me out of the lab."

I chuckle. "It's been a stressful week. I appreciate the compliment."

"I'm sorry. I hope my presence isn't what's causing your stress."

"I'd be a fool if I didn't admit a dead child causes me some anxiety. At the moment, my stress is compounded by the fact that my landlord chose to sell my house to someone else."

"How frustrating! If that happened to me, I don't know what I would do. Of course, I own my house, so that would be all kinds of awkward. Never mind ... I should just shut up now. Anyway, I called because I need to speak to you about Baby Jane Doe as soon as possible."

My heart sinks to my stomach. "Of course. Would you like to meet at Detective Lawrence's office or come to the headquarters of Identity Bank?"

Dakota pauses for a moment. "Nothing personal, but

I'd be more comfortable if we skipped the police department. I've got a few ghosts in my personal life."

"Don't we all?" I mutter. A beat later, I realize that statement could be interpreted many ways. Yet, there's not a lot I can do about it now. I clear my throat. "I'll make sure the conference room is open. See you in a few."

"I'm looking forward to it," she replies softly.

I'm not sure she meant for me to hear that. Rather than answer, I hang the phone up and take a swig of coffee. Something tells me this meeting could change my life.

I enter the conference room with some trepidation. Dakota has paperwork spread out on the table and is writing something.

"I apologize for the delay. One of my former clients was involved in a minor fender bender and it shook her up."

She looks up with a startled expression as she pulls the earbuds out of her ears. "I'm sorry, I didn't hear you. What were you saying?"

"I was just apologizing for being late."

Dakota glances at the clock on the wall. "I was so busy organizing the file, I didn't even notice."

When she closes the file, a whiff of her warm, spicy fragrance reaches me. It's different than the soft floral perfume Cheryl used to wear, but I like it. Suddenly, I'm at a loss for words.

Fortunately, Dakota rescues me. "You look like you're headed toward a firing squad. I swear I'm not that scary."

I take a seat across the table from her and look at her expectantly. "You mean you have good news about Baby Jane Doe?"

Dakota bites her bottom lip before she says, "It depends on your perspective. You are not the source of Baby Jane Doe's DNA."

"I think I told you that."

"You did. But as a scientist, I can't just take people's word for it. I need solid evidence."

"I understand. I get it — but I can't help but feel like I am being punked somehow. I keep looking around expecting to find hidden cameras. Even though I have a basic understanding of DNA, I still don't understand how I got pulled into your case."

Dakota smiles tightly. "I could explain it but it would take charts and graphs and a mini lecture in genetic science."

I pinch the bridge of my nose and close my eyes. "Assuming I believe you and my ex isn't setting me up, what's the short version?"

"That must've been a heck of a breakup if you believe your ex is capable of setting you up for a child murder."

I heave a sigh. "Point taken. It was rough on me, but I doubt Cheryl gives a rip about my feelings. She seems happy in her new life. So, if the DNA test excluded me, what does that mean for Baby Jane Doe?"

"Basically, it means you were not Baby Jane Doe's biological father. However, there is every indication her father was someone related to you."

I stand up and start to pace the perimeter of the conference room. "I know that's what you said before. I've been racking my brain to figure out who it could possibly be."

"Are you sure it's not your brother?"

"I don't think it's Milo. My brother was married for several years. He and Shalonda tried to have a baby for several years. According to my mom, the fertility specialist blamed my brother for their issues. Obviously, I didn't press for details. I figured Milo deserved his privacy — although I still don't know how my mother knows this kind of stuff."

"I get it. Sometimes, family secrets are best left in the dark. But, that certainly puts a different spin on things. Do you think you could have a half sibling out there you don't know about?"

"Negative. Like I said, my parents married ridiculously young. My mom loved my dad with a passion despite his issues. My dad died twenty years ago. Even so, my mother never looked at another guy."

"That's awfully sweet and sad at the same time." Dakota pulls a DNA panel out of the file and studies it intently. "I suppose I could be tracing the wrong branch of your family. It's not unheard of to find an unknown relative a couple of generations back."

"That has to be it. I can talk to my mom and see if she has any more information. I don't have a lot of information about my father's side of the family. After he died, his family blamed my mom for the fact that he drank himself to death. But, maybe she remembers something."

"I'd really appreciate it. I know it's a difficult conversation to have. But right now I'm at a dead end. I hate unsolved puzzles."

"If I don't come up with anything, then what? Is that

poor baby going to end up in some evidence room?"

Dakota's eyes widen. "Okay, I know scientists have a reputation for being methodical and uncaring, but we're not quite that bad. Baby Jane Doe has been buried in a donated coffin. The people of Owl Creek, Tennessee have adopted her as their own until we can figure out who she is."

"I'm sorry. I didn't mean to imply that you or law enforcement lack empathy and compassion. Now that I've been plunked down in the middle of this case, I feel compelled to help you solve it."

"No worries. I am the queen of inarticulation. I'm famous for sticking my foot in my mouth. I guess you'll have to get used to it. I've been updating Dr. Fitzgerald on my progress. He would like me to work with the Cold Case Squadron to see if we can discover Baby Jane Doe's true identity. I have a meeting with the team on Friday."

"I'll have to check with Tristan to see if he wants me to be part of the investigation — that is if I'm allowed to help."

Dakota's cheeks turn a delightful pink. "Umm… I may have insisted on it. After all, you were definitively cleared based on your DNA and your military service overseas. You could not have been involved in Baby Jane Doe's death. Since she is part of your family, your continued involvement is imperative."

Her simple words hit me like a punch to my gut. Whatever happened to this poor innocent child, she was family.

# CHAPTER FIVE

# DAKOTA

As the surrounding chatter grows louder, I glance around the large conference table and surreptitiously wipe my sweaty palms on my skirt. I take a deep breath and try to focus on my job. It is far too people-y in here for me. I much prefer working with data and computers.

My expression must've given my panic away. A young man with tousled brown hair nudges me and whispers, "Breathe before you pass out. I know the group is overwhelming at first. Don't let that bother you. We are like an overgrown family on this team."

I swallow hard. I didn't realize I was being so transparent. "Hi, I'm Dakota Crenshaw. I'm here to provide DNA analysis."

He grins widely. "I know who you are. My fiancé has been talking about you and what you do since the day you guys questioned Nick. I think she has a girl crush on you."

Pauline throws a pencil at him. "Toby! You weren't supposed to tell her that." She looks over at me and winks. "He's not wrong. It's kinda like meeting a superhero in real life. My math skills are abysmal, so I'm gobsmacked that anyone would actually like it."

I feel my cheeks heat. "It's kind of you to say that. You know, I envy you too."

Pauline's eyebrows rise as she asks, "You do? Why?"

"You are at ease in your own skin and you seem to be able to talk to everyone."

"Everyone on the team has their own strengths and weaknesses. For example, Toby over here can make magic happen with a computer. He even invented a device to keep me safe during undercover operations."

Toby blushes and clears his throat. "It's the least I can do. This cause is important to me."

"Hi, I'm Tristan from Identity Bank. I think you'll find we all bring unique talents and perspectives to the Cold Case Squadron."

I glance down at the floor to collect my thoughts. "I appreciate the invitation. I'm just concerned that I'm taking resources from a child who could be found alive. You know what I mean?"

Toby taps his pen on the table. "I understand where you're coming from. But we chose to take this case because we don't know who Baby Jane Doe is and if she has siblings at risk. I take my work seriously. Several years ago, I was kidnapped by a mentally ill woman and someone took the time to look for me. I'll never forget that as long as I live."

My stomach flops. "You're right. I didn't consider the possibility there could be other children."

An older gentleman speaks up. "My name is Frank. I am a former criminal profiler. As such, I can confirm that if one child was killed, others may be at risk. What do you know so far?"

I briefly catch Nick's gaze before I continue.

"Turns out I don't know as much as I thought I did. I first contacted Mr. Weston because I believed Baby Jane Doe could be his daughter. DNA tests have ruled out that possibility. However, they still point to a familial relationship."

An African American gentleman leans forward. "I'm Cody Erickson. I represent Alachua law enforcement along with Pauline Lawrence. Usually, Dylan Palmer would also be part of the team. However, he is knee-deep in another case." Cody turns to Nick. "Nothing personal, but wouldn't Milo be the logical choice?"

Nick shakes his head. "One would think, but it's my understanding Milo can't have kids."

Toby starts rapidly typing on his computer before he glances up. "No other family members?"

"No. It's just Milo and me. Our cousins were killed in Katrina."

"Dakota, where does that leave you?" Toby asks.

"Honestly, very confused. The only thing I can think of is that perhaps I chased the wrong limb of the family tree. If I did, it's a major setback. It took me months of tedious work to come up with Nick. Now, I guess I have to start over again."

Toby gives me a sympathetic look. "That bites. I've been there many times while debugging a program. Would it help if you had a facial recognition program to help you narrow it down?"

I fiddle with my pen as I ponder his question. "The short answer is that I don't know. We may be getting too abstract. After all, there is some speculation when it comes to the computer-generated images based on DNA. Though, we have incorporated Baby Jane Doe's skeletal features into the final results, I'm not sure how true to life it is. Some of these renderings are so close to true life it's spooky. Other times, they seem to be less accurate."

Nick winces. "With all due respect, I'm not sure the DNA findings are all that accurate either. I am not a killer and my brother isn't either."

Tristan clears his throat. "Nick, I know this is tough on you, but you need to ride it out. I'm sure Dr. Crenshaw never intended to wrongly identify the child's killer." Tristan points at Toby. "You get together with Phoenix and see if we can adapt our catfishing software to help Dakota."

"Thank you, sir. I really appreciate it."

"Toby wasn't wrong when he said our Cold Case Squadron is like a large family. You are welcome to call me Tristan. I can access a large pool of investigators if that would be helpful in locating her identity."

"I don't think I need investigators at this time. I just need to retrace my steps to see what I missed."

"I'll assign Toby and Phoenix to provide the required computer expertise to support your mission. Is there anything else you need?"

"I'm not sure you can help with this, but Dr. Fitzgerald wants me to relocate here until the case is finished. Any ideas where I should stay?"

"I like to put folks up at the Sweetwater Branch Inn. It's a local bed-and-breakfast that provides phenomenal food and reliable Internet service. You'll have all the privacy you need. Go ahead and book yourself a room.

Identity Bank will cover the cost for you."

Belatedly, I remember to close my slack jaw. "That's unnecessary. I was just asking for recommendations."

Cody chuckles. "It's best not to argue with Tristan Macklin. He likes to spoil us all and protesting doesn't do us any good. We've all learned to graciously accept the opulence."

I flash Cody a brief grin. "Okay, message received. I won't turn down an offer like that. On a related note, does anyone want to go out for dinner? I hate to eat alone." I hastily glance around the room to watch people's reaction to my offer.

Nick straightens in his chair. "Any other day, I'd be all over a dinner invitation. But, today I think most of us are going to Ketki's birthday party. Pizza and arcade games are on the menu tonight."

"Sounds fun," I concede.

Pauline gasps with delight. "You should totally come with us! I know Ketki wouldn't mind. Do you know anything about video games?"

I snicker. "I was president of the math club at my high school. What do you think?"

"I think Ketki will love you!" Pauline looks at Tristan. "It's been a while since she's had a worthy competitor, huh?"

Tristan nods. "I can't remember the last time Ketki was challenged. This might be fun!"

"Are you sure she won't mind?" I press.

It seems like the whole table erupts in a chorus of "she won't mind" and "this will be awesome." I came here to solve a case. I'm not sure how I got scooped up into the rest of it.

Nervously, I step through the doors of the pizza parlor and look around. Abruptly, a lithe teenager with long black hair marches over. "Who are you?"

"Umm, I'm Dakota Crenshaw," I blurt.

The teenager straightens the sparkly tiara perched precariously on her head. "Do I know you?"

"I don't think so. I'm new in town."

"Not sure how to tell you this, but this is a private party. It's my graduation party."

I smile as a wave of relief passes over me. "You must be Ketki. Nick and Pauline invited me to come to your party. I hear you like to play video games and might be as big a fan of math as me."

Ketki looks at me skeptically. "It depends. How do you feel about losing?"

"Against someone who's better than me? I'm not exactly sure because I don't often lose. I suppose I'd be okay with it if I lost fair and square."

Ketki exclaims, "Game on! I never run into anyone who is as confident in their skills as I am. What games do you like to play?"

"Anything that's challenging, I suppose. But I'm a big fan of a well-designed MMORPG."

"Me too! I like massive role-playing games. You know that Tristan Macklin designs some of the best, right? I'm part of his alpha team."

"Congrats! That's a big honor."

Ketki shrugs. "What can I say? I kick butt at video games. You want to play? Mom says I have to wait until all the guests arrive and we have pizza."

"That sounds like a good plan." I pause to look around. "Are Nick and Pauline here yet?"

Ketki looks at me quizzically. "You know that Pauline's fiancé is Toby, right? They're getting married, but this time I don't have to be in the wedding. At first I was relieved, but then I saw the dresses Pauline chose and I kinda wish I was one of her bridesmaids. Anyway, Nick is a super nice guy, but he doesn't have a girlfriend right now. He's really sad because he broke up with his old girlfriend."

A gentleman with jet black hair and graying temples walks up beside Ketki and places his hand on her shoulder. "Ki, you might let your guest make herself at home before you blindside her with random information."

Ketki glances away. "Sorry, Dad. I just got a little carried away. Dakota is new."

"It's all right," I hasten to assure her. "I knew most of that stuff anyway. I'm working with the Cold Case Squadron to help solve the murder of a child."

Ketki looks at me with wide eyes. "That's way more exciting than a video game."

"Sometimes it can be. I am a forensic genealogist. I study DNA and try to solve cases with genetics."

"So, you're good at math?" Ketki asks.

"As a matter of fact, I'm great at math. But, I'm surprised you caught the connection."

"Isn't DNA all about finding patterns? That's like math to me. It's my favorite thing to do."

I grin. "Can I tell you a secret? Math is my favorite

thing to do too. I have a doctorate degree in statistics from Stanford."

"No way! The only other person I know who likes math as much as me is my stepmom, Shelby. I don't know what to do. I'm supposed to be choosing a college to go to but I can't decide what I want to do."

"I remember feeling the same way when I went to college. But, here's another secret. College is a great place to figure out how you fit into the world."

"Really? I thought I had to know before I picked a school."

"Nope. When I first started school, I thought I would be a math teacher. But after I entered the education program, I realized that I was too shy to be in front of students all day. So, I changed my major to something I felt more comfortable with."

There is a knock on the door and Ketki spins around. "Can we talk later? I gotta get this."

I shrug. "Sure. I'll be here all night."

Ketki opens the door and catches Toby and Pauline mid-kiss. "Eww! You guys are as gross as my parents."

Pauline pulls away from Toby. "Which ones?" she asks with a wink.

Ketki throws up her hands. "All of them! It's like walking into one of Grandma Nancy's soap operas."

Toby blushes. "Sorry kiddo, I didn't mean to embarrass you."

Pauline chuckles. "Just wait until you fall in love, you'll change your tune."

Ketki shudders. "I don't think so. Do you know how many germs people exchange when they kiss?"

Pauline puts her hands over her ears as she and Toby enter the room. "No, I don't know and I'd rather not ever know."

Pauline's face lights up when she sees me. "Oh I'm so glad you made it, Dakota. Our group of friends is the best."

"Pauline, guess what? Jade says that after school is out I can get my first tattoo since I'll be over eighteen," Ketki announces.

"Cool beans! What are you going to get?"

"I think I'll get a colorful feather — "

Ketki stops speaking when someone knocks on the front door again.

"Can somebody else get that? I was traumatized last time."

Since I'm the closest to the front door, I turn to open it. My breath wooshes out as I come face-to-face with Nick Weston. I've only seen him dressed in a shirt and tie. Casual Nick is a whole other animal.

As I'm staring at him, Nick clears his throat. "Well, I guess I don't have to ask if you made it. You look gorgeous!"

I look down at my brightly patterned sundress. "Thanks, I had to get a new dress. I didn't pack appropriately for Florida. It has pockets, see?" I ask as I promptly stuff my hands in my pockets.

"You sound like my mom. Every time she finds women's clothing with big pockets she does a happy dance."

I cringe as I step aside to let him in. "Sorry, I spend too much time in the lab studying files. My conversational skills are a bit rusty."

Ketki shakes her head. "I don't think so. You made me feel so much better. You know, it's funny Nick said I didn't have to have it all figured out either."

"Pizza just came out of the oven!" Ketki's dad, Mark announces.

"I could've told you that," a guy with a service dog yells back.

At my quizzical look, Ketki explains. "That's just my stepdad, John. He's blind, but he's a super good cook. He can always tell when something is done even before the timer goes off. His dog's name is Tuffy."

Nick looks around. "Speaking of dogs, is Lady Gogo here?"

Ketki shakes her head. "No, she's at home keeping Corkscrew company."

I'm lost. But that's not new. Nick walks up behind me and puts his hand in the small of my back as he walks us to the counter where the pizza is laid out.

I flinch. I don't know if my scars are hidden under the thin material of the sundress.

"In case you didn't follow that, Lady Gogo is a puppy Ketki is training and Corkscrew is John's crazy cat with balance problems."

"Umm, okay," I answer. *Way to sound like a functional adult Dakota!*

"Did you get settled into the Sweetwater?" Nick asks.

"I did, but they upgraded me to a suite. Tristan didn't have to do that. I would have been fine at a cheap chain hotel." Nick throws back his head and laughs. "Welcome to the world of Tristan. You're lucky he didn't hire you a limousine to come to the party."

"A limo?" I repeat blankly.

Ketki nods vigorously. "Nick is not kidding. He once flew our entire gaming team to Disney for my birthday. It's just what he does. My advice is to roll with it."

"Roll with it … I suppose that's my new mantra these days."

# Chapter Six

# Nick

I try to hide my amusement as I watch Ketki and Dakota simultaneously stand up and shout at the monitor when another player does something to derail their mission. Dakota is so magnificent when she is facing down a challenge. Her eyes are a mix of fire and joy.

Many people find Ketki's intense demeanor offputting. However, Dakota seems not to mind Ketki's endless questions and commentary. In fact, they are getting along so well they decided not to compete against each other and teamed up to annihilate their competition.

Dakota's unabashed enthusiasm for the game is contagious. Most of Ketki's guests have pulled their chairs around so they can watch the game on the large screen TV.

Suddenly, their score drops dramatically and one of their characters disappears. "Oh man! That sucks! Do you think he did that just because we're girls?" Ketki asks before she groans and sits back down.

Dakota shrugs as she studies the monitor carefully. "I don't know. Maybe he's just a bad player. Or, I suppose it could be a bot."

Ketki shakes her head. "No, Tristan didn't design it that way. All the players are real. Either he's trying to sabotage us or he is an idiot."

Dakota's fingers fly over the controller with lightning fast precision. "No worries. We've got him covered. It's all about girl power, right?"

Ketki shouts with glee as the game announces that the mission is complete and proclaims their team to be the winner. "That was genius! How did you know that gateway was there? I helped Tristan design the game and I didn't know that shortcut."

Dakota pushes her blonde hair out of her face and grins at Ketki. "I play a lot of video games. Usually there's a pattern. So, part of it was instinct and the other part was pure luck."

Ketki sets her controller down. "You can play with me anytime. I don't like saying this, but you're actually better than me."

Dakota graciously shakes Ketki's hand. "Thank you for saying that, but I'd say we're pretty evenly matched. I am quite a bit older than you. I've literally grown up with the gaming industry. In a few years, you'll be able to totally obliterate me." Dakota turns to me. "Do you play?"

I shake my head. "Only flight simulators. That was more like occupational training."

"I thought you were a bodyguard," Dakota replies.

"I am now. But I used to be a chopper pilot in the military."

"Wow! I'm sure that was dangerous. Thank you for serving."

I shrug. "Turns out flying helicopters isn't as

dangerous as falling out of the sky when you're shot down."

Dakota blanches. "I don't know what to say other than I'm sorry."

I shrug. "Fortunately, I lived. I knew the risks when I signed up. So, that part of my life is forever behind me.

Dakota studies me. "Are you okay with that?"

"As okay as I can be. It's not like I can go back and change history."

Ketki nods. "Wouldn't it be cool if we could? I'd like to invent a time machine so people can go back and change their mistakes."

Tayanita collects the dishes from the table in front of her daughter. "Ketki, Mark says you want to turn this into a dance party. Is he right? That doesn't seem like something you would choose to do."

Ketki shrugs. "Okay, so I thought a lot about this. I did some research and most of the colleges sponsor school dances. I don't want to miss out just because of my autism. I figured I could practice here with my friends."

I watch as Dakota tries to follow the conversation. She seems remarkably unphased by the change in plans. I can't say I feel the same.

"Sounds like a great idea. John and I haven't danced together for a long time. But what are we going to do for music?"

Ketki points at a jukebox in the middle of the pizza parlor. "Dad and Shelby helped me pick out some music. All I have to do is hit the button." Ketki sticks her fingers between her lips, making a piercing whistle. "It's time for a dance party. Grab a partner or just dance alone. I don't care. The only rule is you have to be on the dance floor. It's my graduation, so it's my rules."

I groan audibly. "Ketki, you haven't seen me dance. I might ruin your whole party."

"There's a reason you were invited to this party Nick. I needed someone to dance worse than me," Ketki answers cheekily.

Dakota reaches down and grabs my arm. I have no choice but to stand up beside her. "Come on, how bad could you possibly be? You were a helicopter pilot. You must be agile."

I sigh. "You'd be surprised at the lack of transferable skills. Michael Jackson I am not."

Cody shouts from across the room. "Don't let him fool you. I've seen Nick dressed up as Michael Jackson. He won the look-alike contest."

"It wasn't for my dancing abilities, I can promise you."

Dakota gives me an encouraging grin. "Come on. It'll be fun. I am totally shy. If I can put myself out there, so can you."

I roll my shoulder. "You may be sorry. My mother calls me the most uncoordinated person on the entire planet."

Dakota grins. "That's funny. My grandma says the same thing about me. If nothing else, we should be entertaining, right?"

"If you say so," I answer skeptically.

"I never went to my prom. So, this is my first dance party. Don't let me down."

I glance over at Ketki. "You promise not to videotape this?"

Ketki makes the sign of the cross on her chest. "I pinky swear. Before we start, we need to move some tables out of the way."

Something about her comment strikes me as funny. "Okay, I'm bad but you don't need to rearrange the whole room."

Ketki sighs. "Can't you see the tables are too close together?"

I wink. "I'm just teasing." I walk over and place some chairs on the tables and scoot them toward the edge of the room to make my point. After I help clear out a large space, I turn to Dakota and ask, "Are you ready for Operation Humiliation to begin?"

Although Dakota looks calm, I can see the pulse at the base of her neck beating rapidly. "I'm not sure if I should be excited or petrified," she admits with a grim expression.

"I guess we'll find out." I place my hand at the small of her back and escort her on to the newly created dance floor.

As we wait for the music to start, Dakota blushes. "I'm not sure what's come over me, but I think I'm looking forward to this."

I say nothing, but strangely I feel the same way.

# CHAPTER SEVEN

# DAKOTA

*I'm dancing. Holy cow!* I'm dancing with a virtual stranger and having the time of my life. Despite his protestations, Nick is a surprisingly deft dancer. The last time I danced, I was six years old. My grandmother enrolled me in a ballet class. The teacher discouraged me from continuing after she told my family that I had very little talent but lots of enthusiasm. I've never forgotten those words.

Before tonight, I would've never believed that dancing could be fun. I only agreed to participate in the dance party because I knew Ketki would be disappointed if her friends didn't join her on the dance floor. I have been there too. When my school tried to teach square dancing, no one wanted to choose me. I don't blame them. Back in junior high, my burn scars were raw and just plain nasty. Even so, it felt awful.

At this moment, all that is a distant memory as I relax in Nick's arms and rest my cheek against his muscular chest. I haven't felt this safe in a long time.

"Are you having fun?" Nick murmurs in my ear. His voice is so sexy it gives me goosebumps.

I pull away slightly and look up. "Surprisingly, I am. I haven't danced since I was a kid. It's a lot more fun with a partner."

"You know, I was thinking the same thing. You are the first person I've danced with since my ex-girlfriend got married."

I cringe and move out of the comfort of his arms.

"Oh shoot! I didn't mean it like that. It's just that Cheryl and I dated from the time we were kids. I've never tried to dance with anyone else. This is nice."

"Does your ex-girlfriend know you're still in love with her?" I ask bluntly.

"She's aware of how I feel but she married someone else anyway. I'm still working on wrapping my brain around that concept. Every once in a while, I forget that it's possible to have a life without her. I'm sorry if I made this more awkward than it needed to be. I really am having a great time."

"I understand. Sometimes it's hard to leave your past where it belongs."

"Sounds like you've had your own awful breakup —"

"I suppose you could say that. Every time I think I'm over what happened to me, something little reminds me again of what I went through."

Nick brushes a tear off my cheek with his thumb. "I'm sorry you've had that kind of pain in your life."

I shrug. "It was a long time ago. Most of the time, I try to forget. It turns out dancing in your arms is a good way to distract me from bad things."

Nick smiles. "I have to admit, this was a lot more fun than I thought it would be. I like hanging out with you.

Although the circumstances are tragic, I'm glad you're in my life."

Nick leans down and gives me the sweetest kiss I've ever had in my life. Even though I don't date much, I can feel the chemistry raging between us. When I was younger, I used to read romance novels. I would always laugh when a character said their lips tingled as their blood rushed through their body. Now, I know what those books were talking about. I sigh in contentment as he holds me in his arms. I didn't know what to expect when I came to Ketki's party but this is the best night I've had in a very long time. I'll be sad when it's all over.

"You have everything you need for the slideshow?" Toby asks as I fix a typo in my presentation.

I roll my eyes. "Yeah, I think I'm good if I could only proofread effectively."

"Don't worry about it. It's just the team. I figured showing the evidence photos would be easier using the video projector. That way we don't have to pass around pictures."

"You really think this will help? I'm not even sure who Baby Jane Doe is."

"Remember, we're your team and it's our job to help you figure that out."

I sigh. "Usually I'm the one who has the answers. I don't know why her identity is so elusive in this case. It makes me feel like I haven't adequately done my job."

"Not having the answers is tough. But you never know when the pieces are all going to fall together. It's different in every case. I was kidnapped as a teenager and missing for five years. They were never able to unravel the mystery until my brother met Kendall. That's why I work with Identity Bank and the Cold Case Squadron. I want to help put the pieces together for other families."

I swallow hard. Even though his words are encouraging, I can only imagine what he went through.

"I know we just met, but I have to say I am impressed with the way you've put everything into perspective and use your skills to help other people. I don't think I would cope nearly as well. In fact, I know I wouldn't." I abruptly stop talking as I realize what I admitted.

Rather than pressing me for details, Toby silently waits for me to elaborate. I take a deep breath before I explain, "When I was ten, my father tried to kill my whole family by setting the house on fire. My mother was able to escape with my little brother. Unfortunately, I was caught in the fire. I received burns over thirty percent of my body."

"I'm so sorry that happened to you. Trauma like that changes a person."

"That's true. It changed everything I thought I knew about myself. I have a hard time coping with the idea that the person I loved most in the world tried to kill us all."

"That's a lot to process even when you aren't critically ill."

"So, I know what it's like to think you know the answers and then find out everything you thought you knew about your life was wrong. I think that's why I gravitated toward science. In my world, right is right and wrong is wrong and there isn't much in between."

"Speaking of gray areas, what's your hunch about what's going on with Baby Jane Doe?"

"Honestly, I'm not sure what to make of it. If everything we've been told in this case is true, it makes no logical sense."

"I learned a long time ago that just because we believe something is true about the world, it doesn't mean it is."

Before I can respond to his statement, the rest of the team comes in. "Sorry for being late. I thought we were in the other conference room and I sent out the wrong information," Cody says.

My gaze clashes with Nick's as he takes a seat at the table. "Hi," he mouths. I'll be darned if my cheeks don't heat over such a simple greeting.

Toby goes to the front of the room and turns to face the conference table. "Phoenix and I have been working with Dr. Crenshaw —"

"Please call me Dakota"

"Okay, we've been working with Dakota to glean as many details about Baby Jane Doe as possible. To that end, we have decided to share all of the crime scene photos with this team to see if we've overlooked something."

Frank Schofield nods. "Sounds reasonable. The more information we have the better."

Toby nods toward me. "I'll let you take over from here since this is your case."

My heart starts to race. I know this is a small group of people who have my back, but it still terrifies me to speak in front of a large audience.

"Okay, as you know, Baby Jane Doe was found in a well. The farmer who found her was walking his hunting dogs. They wouldn't stop circling this well so he called the police thinking maybe there was a dog or cat trapped in the well. He never expected to find a body."

Pauline shudders. "I imagine it must've been horrific."

"It was. Fortunately, the farmer didn't stick around for the retrieval of the body. From a scientific standpoint, we lucked out because Baby Jane Doe's body was remarkably well preserved. The medical examiner determined she was between the ages of eighteen months and two years when she was killed. She may have been in the well for a couple of years, we don't really know."

Cody is writing in a small notebook. He looks up and asks, "Any discernible cause of death?"

I shake my head. "Because of her age, the hyoid bone is more flexible. Her cause of death could not be determined because there were no obvious areas of damage on her skeletal remains. The only clues we have are the clothes she was wearing."

I touch the arrow key on the computer and pull up a slide. "Interestingly, her dress did not seem to have any labels so it might be homema —"

Nick abruptly leaves his chair and steps in front of the monitor to get a closer look. Suddenly, my explanation is cut short by the sound of Nick retching and running from the room.

I stand there unable to say anything. This picture is sad, but it's not nearly as gruesome as the rest of the slide presentation. His reaction confuses me.

Tristan stands up. "I'll go see if Nick is okay."

After Tristan leaves the room, Pauline asks all of us, "Does anyone know what just happened? Usually Nick is calm and cool under pressure."

Collectively, we all shake our heads and shrug.

"I know Nick's dad died when he was young. Maybe this is all bringing back terrible memories," Toby suggests.

Just then, Nick and Tristan reenter the room. Nick is holding a wet cloth against the back of his neck.

"Are you okay?" I blurt. "If the pictures are too much, I can just give you a verbal summary later."

"This is the toughest thing I've ever been through since my helicopter was shot down in the Middle East."

I recoil from his words. "I'm sorry. I was just trying to get information on the case. I didn't mean to traumatize anyone."

"Your strategy worked better than you could possibly imagine. I am about to give you a tip that could change my entire life."

Everyone leans forward in their seat.

"My hobby is embroidery," Nick announces somberly.

"Not what I expected, but okay."

"No, not okay. You see that little pattern of pink flowers and butterflies on the yoke of her dress? I made that."

Cody shoots to his feet. "Hold up! Are you saying you know who Baby Jane Doe is?"

Nick shakes his head. "No, I wish I did. But somebody I'm acquainted with must know who she is."

Pauline leans into Nick's personal space. "Seems maybe you weren't totally honest with me earlier."

Tristan puts his hands up in a timeout gesture. "Before you jump to conclusions, you might want to listen to what he has to say."

Nick scrubs his hands down his face and clears his

throat. "Like I said, I like to embroidery as a hobby. I know it's weird, but the supplies are small and portable. Whenever I had downtime in the military, I used to embroider stuff for my mom all the time. She thought it was cute. She would donate my work to the church and they'd make quilts for the homeless and stuff. I never thought another thing of it until today. It looks like I need to have a conversation with my mom. I'm sorry, I don't have any answers for you but it seems like my mom might know something."

"I'm sorry you were dragged into this, Nick. But I trust you to do the right thing," Tristan says as he pats Nick on the shoulder.

"Wish me luck. I'm about to have one of the most difficult conversations of my life."

Before I can think about what I'm about to say, I blurt, "Do you need some company? I can help bring some objectivity to the conversation."

Nick flashes me a weak smile. "Some reinforcement might be nice. My mom likes to change the subject anytime we talk about anything difficult."

"I totally understand. Whatever you need, I'm here for you."

Toby turns off the monitor. "I guess Dakota and Nick have a plan. The rest of us will hold tight until we hear from you."

"I'm deathly afraid I'm not going to like the answers I get from my mother. But, whatever I find out, you have to know I had nothing to do with this precious angel's death."

"I think we know that, Nick. Otherwise this conversation would be going a whole lot differently and might include a Miranda warning," Pauline states bluntly.

"Promise me one thing — if my family had anything to do with this, make sure they get prosecuted to the fullest extent of the law. Regardless of whether I'm related to them or not, the person who did this deserves to be punished."

Cody stands up, walks over and gives Nick a one armed hug. "You can count on it."

# CHAPTER EIGHT

# NICK

Dakota looks pensive as Tristan's private plane roars down the runway. I can't tell if she is merely a nervous flyer or if she is scared to death to be alone with me.

I can't say I blame her. It's as if I've been thrown into a horror movie and I have no idea what's coming next. Nothing in my history has taught me how to deal with something like this.

Three weeks ago, my biggest problem was a stinging ego. I was butt hurt because my first love married a guy named Bubba. Now, people I love and respect are wondering if I am capable of murdering a small child. I can't even wrap my brain around that concept. Oh, sure … they've been outwardly supportive, but if I was in their shoes, I would be skeptical too.

Dakota's soft question interrupts my self-reflection. "What are you planning to say to your mom?"

"Heck if I know! It doesn't seem right to go all in without knowing if she even knows what happened. Part of me hopes maybe she just donated my inverted panels to the mission or something and all of this is coincidental."

"It would be nice if that was true, but that theory ignores the biggest piece of evidence we have."

I flinch. "I haven't forgotten about the DNA. For now, I'm ignoring it because I don't know what to think. I know I don't know anything about this child, but I don't have any way to prove that."

"The way I see it, the DNA proves you are not Baby Jane Doe's father. Unless you're covering for a family member, you don't have any reason to lie to me."

"I'm not lying to you seems like a pathetic response to all of this. It's so weird. I am a bodyguard. I observe people for a living. Yet, I am clueless. It's not a comfortable position to be in."

Dakota peels the label off the iced tea she's holding. After a moment, she replies, "I'm sorry for dragging you into this. For what it's worth, I believe you don't know what happened to Baby Jane Doe."

I reach out and put my hand on her forearm. "I'm sorry. I didn't mean to sound bitter. This isn't your fault. You're just trying to figure out who she is. I'm just frustrated because I don't know the answer. On the other hand, I'm afraid to find out the truth."

Dakota swallows hard. "The truth can destroy your entire reality."

"You sound like you have firsthand knowledge."

Dakota's eyes dart away. But before she turns her head, I see tears form. "When I was a kid, my dad tried to kill my whole family. I almost didn't make it."

I try to cover a startled cough. "Wow!"

"Yeah, wow is right. But, it got even more soul shattering. I was in such severe condition the doctors determined I needed a blood transfusion. That's when I discovered the person I thought was my father never was. It turns out my mom isn't related to me either. I was adopted and my parents kept it a secret from me. So, as you can see a little bit of truth can destroy everything you thought you knew."

I shake my head in disbelief. "I hope what I find out isn't nearly as life-changing. How did you survive all that?"

"Because I also learned something else, knowing the truth can set you free. In my case, we found out the person I thought was my father was actually a serial killer. He murdered his other family before he met my mom. I was relieved Sheldon Harper turned out to be a complete stranger."

I scrub my hand down my face. "I already know I'm not likely to be quite so lucky. DNA has already established I have some relationship to Baby Jane Doe. That kind of nails my fate."

"I know it's hard to contemplate that your family may have kept secrets from you. If they have, try to remember you are not defined by what you didn't know about yourself."

I sigh. "I hope that's true. I have a feeling I'm going to find out some things about my family that I never, ever wanted to know as long as I live."

"There's no use stressing over what we can't control. Tell me a little bit about your family."

"Well, much like you, I lost my dad when I was a teenager. He died of alcohol poisoning. It destroyed my mother and sent my big brother into a tailspin. We are only a year apart. When we were younger, we used to be the best of friends. After our dad died, Milo changed. He became ferociously angry and self-destructive. Worse yet, he blamed my mom for my dad's death. That hurt my mother even more."

"Is that why you said you don't get along anymore?"

I nod. "My mom was going through enough garbage trying to support all of us and grieve dad's death. She didn't need Milo to pile on. We had a huge fight where I called him a selfish, entitled jerk. Things have not been the same between us since then."

Dakota blows out a breath. "I'm sorry to have to ask this, but do you think your brother could have changed to the point where he would kill a child?"

"I honestly don't know. Before this happened, I would've sworn up and down Milo couldn't have done anything wrong. After all, I thought this was all a cruel hoax thought up by my ex-girlfriend. Maybe I'm not the best person to try to figure all this out."

"Hopefully, your mom will be able to give us some answers that make sense."

"I hope so. But then again, I hope she doesn't know anything about it."

I nervously wait on my mom's front porch. Very little has changed since Milo and I were kids. In fact, if I look in the garage I'm sure I'll find our childhood bicycles. The squirrel feeder I made her in high school is still hanging from the rafters.

I hear my mom's cocker spaniel barking his head off.

Suddenly, the door swings open and my mom gasps.

"Nicky, what are you doing here? I thought you had a job watching out for some rich folks."

"Mom, that hasn't changed. I still work for Tristan and Identity Bank. My friend Dr. Crenshaw and I are here to ask you some important questions."

My mom's jaw goes slack when she sees Dakota. I don't blame her. Dakota is a stunning statuesque blonde with an amazing smile. I have much the same reaction every time I look at her. "Are you dating your doctor, son? I thought you were waiting for Cheryl to change her mind."

The tips of my ears burn. "Mom! I'm not dating anyone," I insist. "Dr. Crenshaw is just a colleague."

"Colleague? Does that mean you're her bodyguard like in that Kevin Costner movie?"

Dakota graciously steps forward and extends her hand out for my mother to shake. "No ma'am. I'm not famous enough to need a bodyguard. I'm just a forensic genealogist."

"What does that mean?" my mom asks.

"It means I'm a scientist. I study DNA and genetics to try to help solve crimes."

"Crimes?" My mother pins me with a withering glance. "Nicholas Weston! I taught you better than to get mixed up with the law like that. The police shoot people who look like us."

"Oh, I'm so sorry I gave the wrong impression. Your son is helping me solve the case. Nick hasn't done anything wrong. He has been incredibly generous with his time and knowledge. In fact, he's been a perfect gentleman."

"If you're not here about Nicholas, you must be here about Milo. What did he do?" my mom demands.

"I'm not sure either of your sons have done anything. I'm merely investigating."

My mom sounds indignant as she huffs, "Investigating what?"

"You mind if we come in? We can explain it better if we can sit down and talk."

My mom steps aside, but pauses to add, "Wipe those feet."

After we dutifully comply, I escort us all over to the dining room table. My mom gestures toward the table and addresses Dakota. "I'm so sorry this is messy. Someone I know didn't tell me he was coming."

"Don't worry about it, ma'am," Dakota responds. "Mine is much worse because I live by myself with my cat, Mr. Pawsome."

"Call me Thea. Now, what is this about?"

Initially, I was planning to have Dakota explain the science. But my impatience to get to the truth takes over. "Mom, you remember when I used to send you embroidery pieces?"

"Of course I do. They were positively lovely. The women in my church group loved to get them for their quilts. I can't tell you how many times your pieces became the center squares."

"What about the piece I did with the pink flowers and butterflies?"

My mom shrugs. "Shalonda wanted it, so I gave it to her. I didn't think you'd mind. You know how your brother's wife loves flowers. She was here the day it came in the mail. As soon as she saw it, she said she adored the butterflies and needed the panel for something special."

As I look over at Dakota, I can feel the color drain out of my face. My heart starts to pound. "Did she say what she was going to use it for?"

My mom shakes her head. "It's just like I told you. Shalonda told me she needed it for something special. It was the oddest thing though. A few weeks later, I went to go pick up my medicine from the pharmacy. You know, old Mr. Solomon? He told me I was going to love the dress his wife was making for my granddaughter. I just chalked it up to his senile memory. He knows I don't have any grandkids. The man goes to church with me every week."

Dakota studies my mom intently. "Thea, this is critically important. Do you know for sure you don't have any grandchildren?"

"What kind of crazy question is that? Of course I don't have any grandkids. Don't you think I'd know something like that?"

"Look, Dakota is working on the case of a little girl around two years of age who was murdered. Her genetic studies have brought her to our front door."

"What do you mean?"

"Dakota is a scientist who helps match DNA samples to genetic databases to solve crimes. Whoever Baby Jane Doe is, her genes say she's related to us."

"I don't understand. My boys would never hurt a child."

"I'm not trying to say your boys have ever done anything wrong to this child, I'm just trying to give her a name. Do you have any information that might help me?" Dakota pleads.

"So you're telling me there's a dead baby somewhere and she's kin? That's crazy!"

I stand up, walk over and place my hands on my mom's shoulders. "That's what I thought too. When Dakota came to me with this information, I didn't want to believe it. In fact, I thought Cheryl was playing some sort of elaborate prank on me to make me fall out of love with her. But, this is no joke. Do you have any information that would help us make sense of this mess?"

"No! Unless your father was more of a no good, rotten scoundrel than I thought he was. He was so drunk all the time toward the end I wouldn't put it past him. It wasn't like he was being a good father to you and Milo. Maybe he was out sewing some bad seed. Who knows?"

I hug my mom from behind. "Mom, I know Daddy loved you until his very last breath. He would've never done anything like that."

"Didn't you hear the doctor? She said that little baby is our kinfolk. If it's not yours, and it's not your brother's, that's the only thing that makes sense," My mom insists.

Dakota leans forward and asks, "Do you know for certain Milo is unable to have any children?"

"Well, I wasn't sleeping in their bedroom or anything but Shalonda came to me boo-hooin' about not being able to have kids more than once. I was sad for her, but what was I going to do about it?"

"I understand that must've been awkward. I'm sorry to have to keep asking you questions, but Nick mentioned his cousins passed away in Hurricane Katrina. Do you have any half-brothers and sisters or other siblings Nick doesn't know about?"

"Oh Lordy! I sure wish I did. I miss my little brother something fierce. It's been years, but I still can't believe a stupid hurricane wiped out his whole family. I'm not much for science, but common sense tells you there's no possible way this little girl is a member of our family."

Dakota nods. "I know it seems impossible. I'm still trying to figure out if it's true or if there's some other explanation."

"I hope you don't stop. Every child deserves a proper burial and the parents need a chance to grieve. This just breaks my heart."

Dakota wipes away a tear. "Mine too. That's why I've been fighting so hard to figure out who she is. I'm sorry your family got caught up in this."

"Dakota, it's not your fault," I assure her.

"I know. But sometimes it feels that way — especially since the puzzle seems more complicated now than it ever was before."

I turn to my mom. "We're here anyway, would you like to go out to eat?"

"Heavens no! I just put a roast in the oven. It should be ready in about an hour. Do you want to stay for dinner?"

Dakota smiles. "I'd be honored. The meals at the hotel are wonderful, but there's nothing like a homemade meal. Thank you so much for inviting me."

My mother raises her eyebrow at me. "This one has better manners than your last girlfriend. Maybe you should keep her."

"Mom! I already explained this. Dakota and I are just working on her case together. There is nothing more."

"You can say that all you like, but a mother knows these things. Don't lose hope. Cheryl isn't the only woman in the world"

"What's up, boss? Callie told me you needed to see me," I ask as I enter Tristan's office. I'm always in awe every time I come in here. There are so many computers, it looks like he could launch the international space station from his office.

Tristan digs a file folder out from the stack of work on his desk. He takes a second to scan it before he looks up at me. "I know I pulled you off of your regular work to be on the Cold Case Squadron, but how do you feel about pulling double duty?"

"I dunno. It depends on what you mean. My work with the Cold Case Squadron is important to me. If Dakota is correct, that little girl was a relative of mine and I want to find out who she was."

Tristan nods. "Oh, that goes without saying. But we may have an issue."

I lean forward. Tristan always chooses his words carefully. So if he calls something an issue, it needs to be handled. "What kind of issue?"

"Well, you know everyone who works for Identity Bank undergoes a comprehensive background check?"

I nod stiffly. "Yeah? Did something come back hinky on mine?"

Tristan shakes his head. "No, you're in the clear. This is about Dakota."

"What about Dakota?" I ask with trepidation.

"Phoenix was looking through her background check and found something alarming. Has she told you her father is in jail?"

"She mentioned it. Why? Dakota is nothing like her dad."

"Apparently he just got paroled."

"Please tell me you're kidding From what I understand, he was a complete deadbeat. He tried to kill Dakota and her mom."

"Apparently, he's still on the same mission all these years later. He made some specific threats against Dakota."

"Do Dakota, her mom, and her brother know about this?"

"I don't know. It doesn't indicate that in the file. Until we know more, I would just like you to be vigilant."

"Okay, I'll treat her like she's the primary. I still wonder if we should tell the family about the threat."

"I thought about that. But, I don't want to dilute Dakota's focus on this case. So, since Aidan isn't touring, I'm going to pull Jonathan and assign him to watch Allison and Jason Crenshaw. With you covering Dakota, we should be able to respond to any threat."

"I gotta say, I'm not sad about the opportunity to be around Dakota more often. But I hate the circumstances."

Tristan stands up and shakes my hand. "I understand. As Isaac would say, just watch your six while you're watching hers."

# Chapter Nine

# Dakota

"I've missed your face, gorgeous."

I stick my tongue out at Jamie. Even though we are on a video call, he receives the message loud and clear.

He puts his hands up in a gesture of innocence. "What? I was just stating an obvious fact."

I reach up and pat the ponytail at the back of my head. "Jamie, I'm hardly looking glamorous today, besides won't Hannah, Heather, Helen or Hazel, or whoever you're dating get jealous?"

A bleak expression crosses his face. "We broke up."

"Oh you poor thing; you liked her a lot."

Jamie grimaces. "Apparently not enough. I called her by the wrong name. Somehow, she took offense to that."

"I warned you to give up your habit of dating your way through the alphabet."

Jamie nods. "I'm thinking of moving to another letter. How many women out there have names which start with I?"

I chuckle. "I hope someday you come up with a system

which actually works because even though you pretend not to be, you're a pretty nice guy."

"Mmm–hmm, too bad for you. I've already worked my way through the D's."

"You're an ambitious young man — emphasis on the young. However, apparently you have a slight memory problem. I wasn't interested in you the first time you worked your way through that particular letter."

"You can't blame a guy for trying."

I yank my ponytail tighter as I scowl at him. "Can we focus on the real problem here? I can't find a resolution to this case which makes sense. Something is wrong and I can't put my finger on it."

Jamie shrugs. "Give me a couple days and I'll double check your work to see if I find anything amiss."

"This case is going to give me an ulcer. Two days seems like forever."

"Sorry. I'd jump on it sooner except Fitzgerald gave me a priority case. Eventually, you'll probably be on it too. We may actually have to meet in person to go over the files."

I grin. "Are you sure you're not just in it for a free trip to Florida?"

Jamie shrugs. "Maybe. I'll never tell. As far as the boss knows, it's all for work."

"Okay, just send me a text when you need the file."

"Will do. Talk to you later."

After he hangs up, I bury my face in my hands. I'm so frustrated I could cry. I know Jamie thinks I'm kidding about the ulcer part, but I seem to have an almost constant stomach ache now.

I jump when my phone rings. I snatch it up and put it up to my ear. "What do you want now Jamie?"

"Dakota Crenshaw, don't you know your mother's name?"

I blush even though my mom can't see me. "Sorry Mom, I thought you were my coworker. Jamie's getting on my last nerve today."

"Why? Usually you and Jamie have a good time together."

"Yeah, I know. I like teasing him. But I'm just not in the mood."

"What's wrong, baby?"

I pause for a moment trying to determine how much to disclose. "I don't know if you can help. I'm just stuck on a case. I thought I had a lead, but it seems to have evaporated into thin air. Now, I don't know if I'll ever find out who this missing person is."

"Are you trying to do one of your DNA matches?"

I smile. Science was never really my mom's forte. She totally doesn't understand what I do even though I've explained it a million times. "I'm trying to identify a missing person using DNA."

"Oh my, that sounds serious."

"It is. You know how I love puzzles, but I feel like I'm beating my head against the wall with this one."

"I'm sure you thought of this, but is your missing person adopted? Maybe that's why the DNA doesn't match."

"Yeah, I guess that's a possibility. Not everyone knows they're adopted."

"That was a little mean, Dakota. Your dad and I did the best we could. The pastor said because of the unique circumstances of your adoption, it would be better for your self-esteem if we didn't tell you. I'm sorry if that was the wrong decision."

I sigh. "I'm sorry mom. I'm just really tired. I didn't mean that to sound like a criticism. I was just stating a fact. Thank you for the reminder. It gives me another direction to pursue."

"Okay, I understand. I just called to see if you were coming home for my birthday. Sixty is kind of a big deal."

I slap my forehead. "Geez, Mom! I'm sorry I forgot your birthday is coming up. I'm actually in Florida on assignment. I don't think I'll be able to come this year."

"That's all right. I'll just go play bingo with my friends. We found a church that gives really good prizes. Did I tell you I won some gardening tools last time I played?"

I snicker. "No, I don't think you mentioned it. Congratulations!"

"Dakota, you sound tuckered. You should get some sleep. You can't worry about work twenty-four hours a day."

"That sounds like a wonderful idea. I think I'll go back to the hotel and take a bubble bath. I need to get out of my head."

"Just don't forget you have an important job to do," my mom cautions.

"You know me. My job is never far from my mind."

"I hope you find what you're missing in life."

"Shouldn't that be who — since I find people?"

"All I'm saying is you need to be prepared for whatever

you find even if it's unexpected."

"Thanks, Mom. I need to get back to work now."

"Good luck sweetie, I love you."

"I love you too, Mom."

My eyes pop open when I hear a ringing sound. As I sit up, I realize I fell asleep at my desk again.

"Hello," I murmur sleepily.

"Dakota?"

"Hi Nick, yeah it's me. I just haven't had coffee yet this morning."

"Oh shoot! I didn't mean to call so early. I can call back later if you want."

"No, I'm awake now. What do you need?"

"Well, Pauline put a message out on Facebook that today's the day."

"Day for what?"

"She and Toby are getting married today."

"Isn't that the kind of thing you plan for years in advance?"

"Apparently not if you're Pauline."

"That's incredibly brave or shortsighted depending on how you look at it. Why are you calling me?"

I hear Nick pause for a moment before he mumbles to himself, "I should've listened to my first instinct. This was a really, really, really bad idea."

"What's a bad idea?"

"Okay, hear me out before you decide I'm a huge idiot. The last wedding I went to involved my ex-girlfriend marrying another guy. I want to support Pauline and Toby because they are good friends. I just don't know if I can face another wedding by myself. I was hoping you could come with me."

I look down at my nightshirt adorned with Garfield the cat. "You have to give me more details. When does this shindig start and what is the dress code?"

"Clothes," he answers succinctly. I hear some taps on the keyboard. "It says here it's starting at six o'clock, after the art gallery closes."

"'Clothes' is not a specific enough answer. Is this black-tie?"

I can hear the amusement in Nick's voice. "There might be someone there wearing a black tie, but I wouldn't guarantee it."

"Funny. All I'm trying to do is decide whether I have something to wear."

"They are holding their ceremony at an art gallery that has art studios attached. I doubt you'll see any ball dresses unless Pauline is wearing one. The dress you wore the other day was stunning. That would work."

"Oh wow! That's a lot of pressure. I don't even have a gift or anything."

"Don't worry about it. Toby and Pauline are asking for people to donate to his sister-in-law's charity, Locate My Heart."

"Okay, I can do that. What time do you want me to be ready?"

"Ivy's art gallery is a little ways out of town. So, you

should be ready by four thirty."

"I hate to ask this, but who is Ivy?"

"As soon as you are introduced to everyone, it will make more sense. But Ivy is Tristan's sister-in-law. Tristan is married to Ivy's twin, Rogue."

"That sounds complicated."

"It's even more complicated than that. Ivy is married to Rogue's boss, Marcus."

"Are you sure they want me there? I'm pretty much a stranger."

"No more than I am. The thing about this group is once you are tangentially connected to someone, you're in. Since I work for Tristan, this is my tribe. Don't worry, if you're connected to me, you'll be welcomed like an old friend."

"This assignment is turning out to be the most bizarre thing I've ever been through. I can't believe I'm going to Pauline's wedding. I just met everyone a few weeks ago."

"I'm glad you decided to honor your personal mantra of rolling with the punches. I'll see you in a few hours."

I hang up and wonder if I dreamed the whole thing. Then I check my email and find a personal invitation from Toby and Pauline. Well, if nothing else, a nice wedding should get my mind off the case.

# CHAPTER TEN

# NICK

I put a blanket down on the seat in my freshly detailed Jeep. I can't believe I worked up enough nerve to actually ask Dakota to go to a wedding with me. The last time I was this nervous, I was taking Cheryl to the senior prom.

I cringe when I have that thought. I almost blew it last time because I mentioned Cheryl. I don't want to have a repeat performance.

It was all I could do not to press Toby and Pauline about the details of their wedding. I hope they have a dance floor. I had a blast at Ketki's impromptu dance party and I'd like to ask Dakota to dance again now that I have a little more self-confidence.

I hop out of my Jeep and nervously ring her room number from the phone in the lobby. I can hear the smile in her voice when she says, "Right on time. I'll be right down."

When the elevator doors open, my eyes widen.

"You look magnificent," I blurt. "I think I'm underdressed now. That dress is stunning!"

She twirls around in front of me. That's when I notice

her entire back is exposed by the bluish silver couture dress. There is a lacy pattern of scars covering her entire back and some areas are raised and red. I know she mentioned she had been burned in a house fire, but internally I cringe when I consider how much pain must've been involved.

"Isn't this gorgeous? This dress was designed by the manager of the Sweetwater. Matilda even convinced her daughter to give me a discount. It's perfect. I've never had a dress like this before. It is so far outside my comfort zone. Usually, I don't wear anything that exposes my scars, but I couldn't resist this."

"You made a great choice. That dress looks like it was made for you."

"Wait, it gets even better —"

I grin. "Let me guess … pockets?"

She beams at me. "Absolutely! That's what sold me. When you go to a wedding, you have to have a place to put a Kleenex."

"You think there's going to be a bunch of crying at the wedding?" I ask with a note of horror.

She pats me on the sleeve. "Of course, all good weddings require three things."

"Dare I ask?"

"Lots of happy tears, delicious cake and pretty pictures."

"What about dancing?" I prompt.

Dakota smiles wistfully. "Okay, I stand corrected a great wedding requires four things — or maybe five."

"What's the fifth?"

"A dashingly handsome date. I feel like I've hit the

lottery."

My face heats, but I can't think of a single coherent thing to say.

As Dakota and I enter the art gallery, Toby is standing by the door to greet us. "Congratulations, Toby!"

"I'm not sure I deserve any congratulations. Pauline is the one who pulled all this together," he admits with a shy grin. "Personally, I'm just glad to have the whole thing almost finished. Just thinking about being in front of everyone gives me a panic attack."

Dakota smiles. "I am a total introvert too. If I ever get married, I might have to do it online or something. I understand you guys have been engaged for a while. Why did you choose today as 'the one'?"

Toby shrugs. "Logistics mostly. My parents are in Florida because they just got back from a cruise. Since they live so far away, Pauline decided to throw the wedding while they are in town."

Dakota cringes. "Kudos to you. I'm not sure I could deal with the chaos."

Toby nods. "Chaos is definitely the word for what's going on. I just met Crystal, the person who is going to officiate the wedding this morning. She's a notary in Tori's office. I didn't even know you could get married by a notary. But Pauline, Tori and Cody all assure me it's legal. So, I'm just gonna roll with it."

Toby's brother Jameson comes around the corner and beckons Toby. "Your bride-to-be is going to be really ticked off at me if I don't get you in some of the wedding pictures."

Toby looks like he would prefer to fall through the floor. "Gotta go. Again, thanks for coming."

Tristan told me his sister-in-law was a very talented multimedia artist but this is nothing like I've ever seen. Next to the podium at the front of the room is a wire sculpture of Pauline and Toby. Usually, I'm confused by abstract art. But somehow, you can see the passion depicted between them.

Dakota nudges me. "Isn't that beautiful? You can just see how Pauline is taking away Toby's pain. That's the most unique thing I've ever seen. It beats flowers any day of the week."

A woman with Dolly Parton hair and sky high stilettos walks up to the podium. "Hi y'all! Isn't this wild? If you're here, I'm going to assume you're friends of Toby or Pauline – or most likely both. Since these two lovebirds have fallen in love, you rarely see one without the other. Don't get me wrong, that's just how it should be. So, I am a notary. That qualifies me to marry people. What a perk of the job! The only way I could feel more official is if I had a black robe — but black really isn't my color."

The audience laughs at Crystal's antics. Well, everyone except Pauline's father, Desmond. He looks petrified. I've gotten to know the former detective pretty well over the years. He is fiercely protective of his daughter. This has to be amazingly difficult for him. He is clutching her hand like he never wants to let go.

Crystal flips through some papers on the podium. "So,

you might've guessed that this ceremony is going to be unlike anything you've ever seen. Pauline and Toby have assured me that's entirely fine with them. First, I'd like to introduce Declan Ailín. He is a recording artist with Silent Beats records and he is going to sing for us this evening." Crystal grins mischievously. "Okay, so here's the thing. Toby knew all about that part. But what he doesn't know is that Pauline arranged for Mindy Whitaker-Fischer and her husband, Elijah Fischer to accompany them."

Declan walks over to the middle of the stage and high fives Mindy. "Aren't weddings the greatest?" He steps in front of the microphone. "Tonight, I'll be singing a Joe Cocker classic, *You Are So Beautiful.* Toby asked me to sing this song because if he could carry a tune in a bucket, this is what he would like to sing to Pauline."

Dakota snuggles against my shoulder as she sighs. "This is so romantic! I wish some guy would do something half as sweet for me."

Declan, Mindy, and Elijah play their acoustic guitars as Declan sings the soulful ballad. I totally understand where Toby is coming from. Dakota is the picture of sophistication and pure beauty as she sits beside me and watches with rapt attention. When her eyes tear up, I reach into my jacket pocket and pull out a tissue. She shoots me a grateful smile which makes me feel like a total hero.

When Declan concludes his song, they transition into the wedding march as they gracefully leave the stage and sit in the front row while they continue to play.

As Pauline and her father walk up the aisle, it is slow going because of Desmond's gunshot injury he obtained while serving as a police detective. When they reach our row, I overhear Pauline. "Thanks for setting the standard so high for how a man should treat me, Dad."

I swear I see Desmond's eyes glistening as he turns and flips Pauline's veil over her head. He gently kisses her cheek. "You deserve the best and I think you found him."

Toby is struggling to contain his emotions as he walks down the stairs and offers his elbow to Pauline.

Pauline turns to face Toby at the front of the room in her sleeveless mermaid dress. Dakota whispers, "Is that a blood glucose meter on Pauline's arm? I never realized she was diabetic."

Since I know the story behind the device, I respond, "Just wait."

Crystal wipes away tears. "I don't know about all of you, but I'm not sure if I'm going to make it through this wedding. Everything is so beautiful. Fortunately for you, I'm only the administrative support for these nuptials. So, I'm going to turn it over to Pauline and Toby."

Pauline's veil falls over her arm. Toby notices and brushes it back. When he does, he sees the device on Pauline's arm and reaches out to touch it. Understandably, he tears up.

Pauline leans into the microphone "Can I go first? I've been thinking about this for what seems like forever." Toby gestures for her to continue.

"I don't think anyone would be surprised to know I started falling in love with you long before we were ever dating. At first, I was infatuated with your astounding level of handsomeness."

Toby blushes and pulls at his shirt collar. "If you say so."

Pauline grins. "I *do* say so." She places her hand over the device on her arm. "I've liked you for a really long time. But, I truly fell in love with you when you objected to me going on an undercover mission with every fiber of your being. Yet, when it came down to it, you understood that I had to solve the case — even if it cost me everything. You didn't keep me from being me, you moved heaven and earth to create a way for me to stay safe while being true to my oath as a police officer."

Toby reaches out to wipe away a tear on Pauline's face. She turns to the audience. "For those of you who don't know the story, Toby created this little device to fool some evil human traffickers. It allowed him to communicate with me without being caught. In the end, we freed a bunch of girls and gave them a new lease on life. I was only able to do my job because Toby loved me enough to let me fly while keeping me anchored."

"It was the least I could do. I love you."

Pauline reaches up to remove the device. Toby's eyes widen when he sees a replica of the device tattooed to Pauline's arm.

"You hate needles! I can't believe you did that."

Pauline shrugs. "It wasn't as bad as I thought it would be. I just wanted something tangible to remind me of exactly when I fell head over heels in love with you. It was when you put my well-being ahead of your well-founded fears. After that, I knew no matter what happened, you'd always have my back. Tobias Payne, I will love you forever and a day. Please marry me."

The corner of Toby's mouth hitches up. "I'll marry you today and every other day until the day I die."

Everyone in the audience erupts in a chorus of awws. He looks out into the audience until he finds Jade Ailín. "I take it my favorite tattoo artist has been a little busy."

Jade shrugs. "I like putting meaningful art on my

friends. That's what we do at Ink'd Deep."

Pauline watches in horrified, nervous anticipation as he removes his bowtie and starts to unbutton his shirt. "I don't think we're supposed to be at that part yet," she says in a stage whisper.

"Trust me?" Toby replies softly.

"Every single day of my life."

"I'm glad you said that. I have something to show you too." Toby pulls the front of his dress shirt to the side to show a tattoo right above his heart.

Pauline gasps. "You covered your scar with Ivy's sculpture."

"When you found me, I was a shell of the person I was supposed to be. I had been kidnapped for five years and didn't know how to put my life back together. At first I was completely embarrassed at my weaknesses. But, then you started showing me that being open and honest is its own special kind of strength. Loving you has helped me put that dark episode in my life back in the shadows where it belongs."

"It's not hard to love you Toby Payne. To me, it comes as naturally as breathing."

Toby tearfully nods. "I feel the same way about you. I used to think I had to hold onto my fear and pain to keep me safe from the darkness in the world. You showed me that wasn't true. What happened to me wasn't my fault, so there's no need for me to keep a visible reminder of my assault and kidnapping. You help me keep the past buried and encourage me to live my best life. Pauline Lawrence, will you accept me with all my quirks and flaws and be my wife forever?"

"If you accept that I will forever jump into things with

both feet without looking, I'll overlook the little things like the fact that you put milk in your cereal bowl before your Cheerios. I love you Toby Payne and I look forward to spending forever with you."

Crystal waves her hand in front of her face like she's trying to fight back tears. "If no one objects, let's say we get these two lovebirds married. Clearly they are perfect for each other."

When I glance over at Dakota, tears are streaming down her face. I take another tissue from my pocket and silently hand it to her. She startles when it touches her hand, but her teary smile makes me want to move heaven and earth to see it again.

After a few beats of silence, Crystal makes a gesture of wiping sweat off of her forehead. "Longest forty-five seconds of my life. I don't know what I would've done if someone would have objected." She squares up her shoulders and looks directly at the couple. "Toby and Pauline Payne, by the power vested in me as a notary in the state of Florida, I hereby pronounce you husband and wife." She winks at Pauline. "Pauline, I know you've been waiting what seems like forever for this day. You may thoroughly kiss your groom."

Pauline looks out at us and winks. "Mr. Payne here is a bit shy. So, to respect that I'll approach this with much more caution than I usually do."

The side of Toby's mouth hitches up in amusement as his eyes light up with mischief. Without any warning, he bends Pauline over at the waist to give her a deep, thorough Hollywood-type kiss. When she stands up with a slightly dazed expression on her face, he quips, "With you by my side, I'm not nearly as timid as I once was. I can't wait to take on life with you, Mrs. Payne."

Pauline does a little happy dance before she searches the audience. "Hey Mom! I did it! I married a guy who loves me for who I am. I am the luckiest woman in the whole world!

I watch as her mom dabs away tears. "You did. You found your perfect Prince Charming and I couldn't be happier for you."

# CHAPTER ELEVEN

# DAKOTA

Nick is cradling me in front of him as we watch the bouquet toss from the sidelines. Pauline scans the crowd and her gaze lands on me. "Hey, Dakota! I happen to know you are as single as they come. Get your booty out on the dance floor."

Reluctantly, I leave Nick's arms and sullenly march to the center of the room. I end up next to Ketki, who looks just as displeased as I feel.

"Can you believe this? Shelby says I'm old enough to participate this year. I am totally not interested in getting married. I don't know why I have to play this silly game."

I nod sympathetically. "I can't tell you how many times I've had to do this in my life. It's better just to get it over with."

Ketki crosses her arms around her body. "Pauline shouldn't be throwing it at us. Where is Lauren? She was planning to get married before Pauline and Toby."

"Who is Lauren?" I ask, a little confused by the non sequitur.

"Oh, you haven't met her, I guess. She's Dylan Palmer's

fiancée.

"Okay, he is a member of the Cold Case Squadron but someone told me he is out of town on assignment."

"He's not just a member of the task force, he is the commander. He met Lauren while he was on a case — sorta like the situation between you and Nick."

I shut my eyes as Pauline throws the bouquet, But laughter in the crowd makes them spring open. I catch a glance of the colorful bouquet as it bounces off of someone's head and lands directly in Ketki's hands.

"What am I going to do with this?" she asks in a horrified whisper as she tosses it toward my unsuspecting hands.

I awkwardly catch the bouquet and cringe. "I don't need it either. I don't even have a boyfriend. I'm certainly not going to get married."

"Nick is your boyfriend. You just don't know it yet. He looks at you the same way my dad looks at Shelby and my mom looks at John. I hate to tell you this, but you're toast."

I glance over at Nick as he talks to Cody and Tristan and decide Ketki is not entirely wrong.

When Nick catches my appraisal, he excuses himself and walks over to me with purpose. My heart beats faster with anticipation. I've always had a thing for tall, dark, and handsome guys. Nick fills the bill delightfully well.

He stops in front of me and reaches out to grab my hand. He kisses the back of my knuckles. "You look like a woman who needs to dance. Shall we?"

I nod mutely, a little overwhelmed by the moment. Nick places his arm around my waist. I flinch when his fingers hit a noticeable ridge in my scar tissue.

When he feels my reaction, he quickly pulls his hand away. "Oh, I'm so sorry. I didn't mean to hurt you."

"You didn't hurt me, I'm just self-conscious. I don't usually display my scars because many people find them distasteful and upsetting."

Nick spins me around in his arms so I'm facing him. His expression is stern. "You shouldn't have to hide yourself because other people feel uncomfortable. Honestly, your scars are disconcerting to me. When I look at them, I feel sorry for the little girl who went through all that pain."

"See? They are upsetting. That's the reason I don't usually dress like this."

"Wait, I haven't told you the rest of my reaction." Nick runs his thumb up my spine. The movement is unexpectedly sensual even though much of my skin in that area is completely numb. "A second after I felt sorry for you, I felt immense pride for the person you've become despite your pain. You are so strong to have survived everything and still function as a wonderfully warm and open human. I'm not sure I would have been able to do the same."

His words cause me to freeze. I debate what to say next. I guess if he doesn't understand, we were never meant to be. "There's something I hate almost as much as being a victim. I don't like being considered inspirational. I just live my everyday life trying to survive like everyone else. I don't do anything terribly extraordinary. I go to work and come home and watch Netflix movies with my cat. In fact, I am the very description of a sad stereotype."

"I understand. I get the same thing when people find out I am a wounded warrior. So, for purposes of clarity,

I'm going to be crass and tell you the first thing that came to my mind when you came out of the elevator today."

I lean forward and rest my forehead on his chest as I brace myself for his answer.

He gently lifts my chin up with the tip of his finger. "I want you to see my face as I'm telling you the honest truth. The first thought which crossed my mind when I saw you tonight was that you are the most perfectly exquisite woman I have ever seen. I wish you could see yourself through my eyes."

I flush bright red from head to toe. "That's probably because you haven't seen all of me. As revealing as this dress is, it still hides plenty of damage."

Nick shakes his head. "Stop it. It's a compliment and you don't have to qualify it. You are beautiful inside and out — scars and all. To say anything else minimizes who you are and that's not okay with me."

I shrug. "I guess I don't see myself the way you see me. I'm smart and abundantly nerdy, but beautiful? Not so much."

"I think we're going to have to agree to disagree. While we're doing that, I think we should dance.

I curtsy. "I think I can manage to do that."

Nick leads me out to the center of the dance floor.

Declan is doing a masterful job covering Ed Sheeran's *Perfect*. Nick leans down and kisses my forehead. "See? Even the music agrees with me."

Jamie looks at me quizzically through the video screen.

"You look different today. Florida definitely agrees with you."

"Yeah. Aside from this pesky case, I'm having a wonderful time here." Without warning, my cheeks heat as I remember the magical evening I just spent with Nick.

Jamie points at me. "You need to spill! I know that look anywhere. Dakota has a crush on someone and I need to know who."

I shake my head at him. "Jamie, you are my coworker. You do not need to know everything about my love life," I tease.

"Aha! You just admitted you have a love life. So, you can't deny it now."

"All right, all right. I went to a wedding and had the most marvelous time. It was like something out of a fairytale. I danced until I got blisters on my feet."

Jamie scrunches up his nose. "Blisters don't sound too magical to me."

"It's because you weren't in my shoes."

Jamie laughs out loud. "Well, That's a good thing because your shoes made you have blisters."

"You're a funny guy. What I meant is I got to set aside everything I thought I knew about myself and become someone's fantasy. It's a powerful thing."

"That sounds vaguely dirty," Jamie quips.

"Oh shut up! I meant I danced away the night like Cinderella and my Prince Charming wants to do it again."

"Dare I ask who your Prince Charming is? You were single when you went to Florida. You've only been gone a month."

"Says the guy who claims to have found Ms. Right after a trip through the drive through at McDonald's."

"Fair enough. But that's kind of the way I operate. You don't jump into things both feet first. That's just not you."

"That was before I met Nick Weston. The man is really good at convincing me to take chances and hope for the best."

Jamie's eyes grow wide and he pauses so long I wonder if our Internet connection is broken. "Nick Weston as in the guy who's DNA we are investigating? Do you think that's prudent? What if he turns out to be guilty of killing that little girl?"

"Trust me, I've thought about it a lot. But Nick's DNA is not a direct match to Baby Jane Doe's. Close, but not a complete match. He has told me what he knows and I believe him."

Jamie grimaces. "Okay, you gotta do what you gotta do. But I'm just telling you, I went over your work with a fine tooth comb. I haven't been able to come up with another branch of that family. So, chances are, one of Baby Jane Doe's relatives is close to Nick Weston."

"Oh trust me, I am aware. Some nights, I think of very little else. You've always told me I have really good judgment. So, my gut instinct tells me Nick is not involved. I might be proven wrong, but I'll cross that bridge when I come to it."

Jamie cringes when he hears my explanation. "Okay, I'm not just saying this as a guy who wishes you were interested in him, I'm saying this is your friend. Be careful! If this job has taught us anything, it's that there are plenty of evil people where you least expect them. I have a bad feeling about this. You are usually far more cautious than this. Are you sure you're not letting your hormones override your natural tendency to be a skeptic?"

I shake my head. "No, I'm not one hundred percent sure of anything. After all, the DNA suggests Nick's family is involved. He could be covering for someone, but I just don't think so. Thank you for double checking my work. I'll keep you in the loop on the case."

"So, that's it? You're just going to ignore my advice?"

"No! I'm not ignoring it exactly, I'm just prioritizing it. I'll be vigilant, I promise."

# Chapter Twelve

# Nick

Due to an overturned truck blocking my commute, I am the last person to join the Cold Case Squadron meeting at Identity Bank. I hate being late, but it was out of my hands. I balance my coffee cup on my notebook as I let myself in the door.

As I settle in my seat, it's clear I missed something important. As if to confirm my suspicions, Tristan walks over to me and asks to speak to me in the hall. For a moment I have flashbacks of being hauled into the principal's office in junior high school.

I prop my foot up on the wall as I wait for Tristan to tell me what is going on.

Tristan rakes his hand through his hair before he meets my gaze. "Nick, you know I value your integrity and commitment to Identity Bank —"

"Am I being fired?" I blurt as my stomach plummets to my toes.

"No. I'm not firing you. But, after today's meeting you might wish you never met any of us. There has been a troubling development. I know you said that it didn't matter who was responsible for Baby Jane Doe's death, you wanted them punished. This is where the rubber meets the road. You may want to excuse yourself from the Cold Case Squadron. I don't want to put you in a position where you have to choose between us and your family. I can assign you another protection detail."

"Over my dead body! I signed on to this to make sure Baby Jane Doe got justice. If that means someone in my family is implicated, I can't turn my back on that. Justice is justice even if it hits close to home."

Tristan put his hand on my shoulder. "Okay, I hear you. But if it gets too intense and you need to leave, I understand that too."

"I appreciate that, but when I joined this mission, I pledged to be part of the team. If I duck out because things get difficult, I'm not much value to anyone."

"Okay, let's go back inside so you can hear what the team has to say."

When I go back into the conference room and take a seat, I realize Phoenix Wolf has joined our meeting via video call. I catch Dakota's gaze and notice she looks stricken. Her expression scares me more than Tristan's cryptic warnings.

Dylan wipes his hands on the thighs of his jeans. "I'm glad we were able to wrap up my other case, but it's difficult to be the commander of the Cold Case Squadron on a day like today." The detective pins me with a level glance. "Although it's difficult, please try to remember that Dr. Crenshaw and Phoenix are just the messengers. They are interpreting data in the best way they know how to help solve this case."

"Okay, quit stalling please. You all are freaking me out.

I'm guessing that you must've discovered Baby Jane Doe belongs to Milo."

On the video screen, I see Phoenix nod. "We won't know anything for sure until we get a definitive DNA match. However, since Toby is on his honeymoon, he asked me to follow up on whether Baby Jane Doe's genome-based projection matches pictures of Milo Weston."

"Where did you get pictures of my brother?" I blurt as the random thought crosses my mind.

Dakota smiles tightly. "Despite her reservations about what we are doing here, your mother was very helpful in helping us obtain pictures of your brother over a wide spectrum of ages. This allowed the facial recognition software to have a higher degree of confidence in the results."

"What results?" I ask, my voice barely above a whisper.

Dakota gives me such a look of pity it causes a chill to go up my spine. "I'm so sorry Nick," she whispers as she pushes a button on her computer.

Briefly, Phoenix disappears from the large wall monitor and a picture of Milo when he was about three appears on the screen next to the computer-generated picture of Baby Jane Doe. It is like a gut punch. Baby Jane Doe is the spitting image of my big brother — right down to the space between her teeth. It is too much to process.

Phoenix's picture reappears as he rejoins the conversation via the video call. "The analysis of all of the pictures we have available of both parties shows that there is a high degree of likelihood that Milo is the father of Baby Jane Doe."

I know what I said about seeking justice, but suddenly

my rage erupts like a volcano. "Based on what? A picture dreamed up in some computer somewhere based on speculation? I know what it looks like, but this can't be right! Everyone I've talked to says Milo and Shalonda weren't able to have kids. There has to be a mistake somewhere!"

Dakota pushes a chunk of her blonde hair out of her face. "I understand you want our analysis to be wrong. Who could blame you? Unfortunately, every piece of data we have points to your brother. I wish I could make that not be true, but facts are stubborn."

"Facts? You don't even know exactly who this child is, where she's from, or even what race she is. So, I'm just supposed to believe my brother is some psycho killer?"

Cody leans forward. "I know this is a tough spot to be in, but if you listen carefully to Dakota and Phoenix that's not what they're saying at all. You've been around law enforcement long enough to know that just because someone is related to a crime victim doesn't mean they committed the crime."

Grudgingly, I admit, "I guess you're right. So now … what do I do with this information?"

Dakota looks like she'd like to throw up. I concur. "I know your family situation is strained right now, but if you have any sway with your brother, can you please try to convince him to submit a DNA sample? Although our results are compelling, it's not enough to get a search warrant."

"Dakota, you've met my mom. This is going to destroy her."

Dakota sighs. "I know. That's why I think you should get Milo ruled in or out before we tell Thea."

"I'll try. Honestly, it's difficult to talk to my brother about average, everyday things. I can't imagine how horrendously this conversation is going to go."

"You won't know unless you try. It sounds like his cooperation is crucial to identifying Baby Jane Doe and finding out what happened to her. Right now, connecting with your brother is your number one priority. Don't worry about your job at Identity Bank," Tristan replies. "It'll be here when you get back."

"I'll try my best. But I make no guarantees."

"That's all we can ask for," Dakota adds.

Impulsively, I ask, "We made such a good road team last time. Do you want do it again?"

Dakota looks befuddled. "Why? Wouldn't my presence make things worse?"

"Please? I don't really want to explain all this by myself."

"I can offer my plane," Tristan adds to sweeten the offer.

Dakota grins. "Who could turn down such a deal? A road trip with one of my favorite guys and swanky transportation."

"You're the best!" I gush.

Dakota winces. "You may change your mind by the time this is all over. Usually, people don't take the news I give very well."

I look around the luxurious hotel suite and whistle softly through my teeth. "I swear he does this just to keep us on our toes. How long does he think we're going to be here? A suite with two rooms and a full kitchen and living room is a bit much for me. I don't think Tristan quite understands that my mom was a single mom for much of my childhood. Being dirt poor meant hotdog buns were a luxury. I ate mine on white bread." I gesture toward the chandelier in the living room. "I've been working with Tristan for years, but this kind of thing still blows my mind."

Dakota spins around in the huge room. "I've never seen anything like this. It's like something out of a movie. I feel bad using Tristan's resources like this. You know how many homeless kids could eat for what a place like this costs?"

"I don't, but I suspect Tristan does. He gives to hundreds of charities every single month. Sometimes, he just does stuff like this to make sure that his employees are comfortable and feel at home."

Dakota chuckles, "I don't know about you, but this doesn't feel like home to me. Of course, I'm single and I live with a cat, so you have to take that into consideration."

"Are you really though?"

She stares at me blankly. "Am I really what?"

Crap! I started this conversation, I guess I better see it through. "Are you still single? I was under the impression we were on our way to being a couple."

Dakota wraps her arms around her body and takes a deep breath. "Under any other circumstances, I would probably totally agree with you. Hanging out with you at Ketki's party and Toby and Pauline's wedding has been amazing —"

My heart skips a beat. "But?" I press.

"Given everything that's gone on in the case, this may

not be the ideal time for us to be together. If this case ever goes to trial and I'm called as a witness, a defense attorney could shred us and imply we tainted the investigation."

"You still think I'm involved somehow, don't you?"

"I don't. But if people found out we're dating, they could come to all the wrong conclusions."

I scowl at Dakota and stand up to pace the room. "You know what this feels like? I'll tell you. It feels like you're just another woman looking for an excuse to ditch me."

"I'm sorry you feel that way. I'm just trying to preserve the integrity of the case so we can find out who Baby Jane Doe is. I'm sorry if that gets in the way of your dating plans. I didn't come to Florida to follow love. I came here to solve a mystery and help a little girl get her identity back."

"I'm not implying your work isn't important," I snap.

She raises an eyebrow. "Really? Because it sure seems like that to me." She turns and starts walking toward her room. "I'll be ready at eight a.m. sharp. I've had entirely too much of today."

With that announcement, I watch her walk into her suite and slam the door. Unless I'm incredibly lucky, she'll probably exit from my life too.

# CHAPTER THIRTEEN

# DAKOTA

After a fitful night of sleep, I can't help but wonder if I've made a terrible mistake. DNA has shown that Nick is not Baby Jane Doe's father. So, even I don't understand why I am putting distance between myself and Nick. Maybe it's not even necessary. However, even as I have that thought I know a defense attorney would have a field day if I was in a relationship with a relative of the person who harmed Baby Jane Doe. Of course, we don't even know yet whether Milo is Baby Jane Doe's father or if he is involved in her death.

As I study my business attire in the mirror, I decide being a confirmed science nerd, bookworm, and cat lady is far easier than figuring out this relationship stuff. I take a deep breath and try to put my game face on. I'm not even sure I have a game face, but for today, I'll pretend I do.

With trepidation, I walk across the suite toward Nick's room and lightly knock. When he answers the door, he is tucking in his ice blue button-down shirt. I draw in a deep breath. The time of day doesn't matter; this man is always breathtakingly gorgeous.

I paste a smile on my face. "Are you ready to go?"

"Just a second, I need to grab my wallet. Do you mind if we stop for coffee? Today, I don't think there's enough caffeine in the world."

I shrug. "Works for me. Do you know how far it is to your brother's house?"

Nick pulls out his cell phone and thumbs through his messages. "According to Phoenix, he works as a warehouse manager about an hour from here."

I swallow hard. "Are you as nervous about this as I am? I could barely sleep last night."

"Honestly? I'm terrified! You know how we talked about that the truth can set you free? The truth can also destroy your whole family. I'm not sure I'm ready for that to happen."

"Try not to jump ahead of the evidence. There may be a simple explanation to all this that we're just not seeing."

"I hope you're right. But, I have this awful feeling things are going to get a lot more complicated soon — and I don't mean just with my brother."

"What do you mean?"

"I didn't sleep much last night either. I spent hours thinking about how today is going to destroy my family."

"I'm so sorry. I wish things were different."

"Yeah, me too. The hours I wasn't worrying about my mom and my brother, I was thinking about us."

When I start to say something, Nick puts his hand up to stop me. "I know you said there is no us right now. I'm not sure I'm okay with that. I never expected to fall for you under the circumstances, yet somehow I did. I don't know how to protect my family, seek justice for a dead little girl, and keep you in my life all at the same time."

I reach out and grab Nick's hand. I pause for a moment to collect my thoughts. "I don't have any answers either. I wish I did. If I had my wish, we would've met at a karaoke bar or something that didn't have anything to do with your family or Baby Jane Doe."

Nick flashes me a grin. "Somehow, I can't picture you at a karaoke bar. It doesn't seem to be your scene."

"Oh, it's not really my thing. I'm just saying in my fantasy, I have the confidence to be someone I'm not and life between us isn't so complicated."

"Do you think life between us will ever get to the point where it isn't hopelessly complicated?" Nick asks as he squeezes my hand.

"I don't know. A lot of it depends on how things work out with your brother. If I have to testify against him, you may not ever forgive me."

"I'm not sure I want to give Milo that much control over my future."

"I don't think we have any choice. If we don't play it safe, whoever murdered Baby Jane Doe might get away with it and as much as I like you, that's not an outcome I can live with."

Nick swallows hard. "So, is this the end of us forever?"

I flinch at the pain in his voice. "I'm not ready to say that. Let's just see what happens next."

As we pull up to the furniture warehouse, my heart is racing. I'm not sure what outcome I am hoping for. If Milo is really Baby Jane Doe's father it's going to be devastating for Nick and his mother. If he's not, we don't have any answers and may not be able to solve the mystery of who she is and how she died.

Nick walks around the car and helps me out. Then, he pulls me in to a brief hug. "Thanks for helping me. If it wasn't for your presence, I would be a total basket case. Let's go see if we can find some answers."

We enter the office and are greeted by a teenager decked out in goth clothing. "Is Milo Weston here?" The stress in Nick's voice is evident.

The teenager shrugs. "Sure. He's getting set to go to lunch, but I think you just caught him."

I glance down at my phone. "It's only ten o'clock. Isn't that a little early for lunch?"

The girl behind the counter smirks at me. "For some people, yes, but if you start work at five thirty in the morning, you tend to eat lunch earlier."

"You're right. I didn't think about that. Anyway, can we please speak to Milo?"

The receptionist taps a button on her phone and picks up the receiver. "Milo Weston please come to the front desk." The sound echoes through the warehouse.

I glance over at Nick. He looks positively gray. If I didn't know better, I'd swear he's about to pass out. "Breathe," I whisper. "It's going to be okay."

"You don't know that for sure," he mumbles as he watches his brother come in the room.

I thought I knew what to expect because I've been studying pictures of Milo for weeks. But in person, he's much more imposing. Nick is tall, but Milo has a few inches on him and he's got muscles like a bodybuilder.

Milo stops at the receptionist's desk. "I swear Erika, if someone else calls in sick today I'm going to start sending out pink slips. I can't run a business this way."

Erika blanches. "Mr. Weston, that's not what this is about. Someone is here to see you."

"Who in the world would come see me at work? We're in the middle of nowhere."

"I don't know sir. I didn't ask their names. They are sitting right over there."

Milo whirls around to face us. When he recognizes Nick, his expression hardens.

"What do you want?" he demands with a sour expression.

"It's great to see you too, big brother," Nick answers sarcastically.

"I haven't seen you in years, so I'm curious why you chose to visit me here."

Sensing the tension between Nick and his brother, I step forward and extend my hand. "Good morning. My name is Dr. Dakota Crenshaw. If you have a few minutes, we need to talk to you."

Milo shakes my hand as he gives me a frank perusal. "Why?"

I scan the room around me and see lots of curious faces. "It might be better if we have this conversation in a private location."

Milo shifts his gaze to Nick. "So what did my brother do this time?"

Nick's hands clench at his side. "Nothing, you jerk."

I clear my throat. "Perhaps it would be more

productive to talk privately," I suggest again.

Nick nods. "Dakota is right. We should take this outside. You have a private place we can go?"

Milo points toward the back door. "It's not much, but would my camper work? It's out back."

I pick up my purse from the seating area. "Works for me."

Milo scowls at Nick. "You better not be wasting my time with something stupid."

Nick heaves a sigh. "You have no idea how much I wish this was something like that."

Milo stops in his tracks. He studies Nick carefully. "You're being serious, aren't you?"

Nick nods as he fights to hold back tears. "I've never been so serious in my whole life."

# Chapter Fourteen

# Nick

When I step into Milo's camper in the back of his pickup, and turn around to help Dakota navigate the steep stairs, I am instantly taken back to my childhood.

Before my dad died, our family would go camping almost every weekend. It's one of the few happy memories of my childhood. My dad loved to fish and we would plan our excursions carefully around fishing season and where my dad had been lucky before. Back in those days, my brother didn't hate the sight of me. At one point in our lives, we used to be the best of friends. My dad's death seemed to change all that. Now, we struggle just to communicate about everyday things. I can't imagine how massively difficult this conversation will be.

Milo quickly converts the bed into a table with bench seats. Dakota is watching with wide-eyed fascination. "I've never been in one of these things. I always wondered how people fit everything in. This is really cool."

My brother appears bewildered by her compliment. He pulls some soda out of a cooler and offers us one. After we all sit down at the table, he pins me with a sharp glance. "Okay, we've done all the polite stuff. Tell me why you're here."

I open the soda and take a long sip as Milo looks at me expectantly. "Okay, there's no way to sugarcoat this and make it easier to comprehend. So, I'm just going to tell you what's up."

My brother's eyes widen with horror. "Is Mom sick?"

I shake my head. "As far as I know, the situation has nothing to do with Mom."

"What 'situation'?" Milo demands.

Dakota sets her soda down and pulls a business card out of her purse. "It's hard to explain without introducing myself. Like I said before, my name is Dr. Dakota Crenshaw. I am a forensic genealogist."

"Like CSI?" Milo asks.

"Not exactly. I use data in publicly available DNA banks to help solve crimes. I tracked down your brother during the course of one of my investigations."

"Dude, I thought she was your girlfriend! I was just about to congratulate you for finally having the good sense to dump Cheryl. I asked this before, and I'll ask it again. What did you do?"

"I didn't do anything. Besides, I didn't dump Cheryl. She dumped me and married someone else."

Dakota nods. "Your brother is not a DNA match to our victim. We're here today to see if we can get a sample to rule you out too."

"Victim! What victim?"

I jump back into the conversation. "There's no easy way to ask this, but we need to know. Did you and Shalonda have any children?"

"What the freak are you talking about? You know we don't have any kids. If we did, Mom would be rejoicing, and the whole Internet would know."

Dakota pulls a file out of her tote bag and hands Milo the side-by-side comparison.

I watch as my brother studies the picture. His hands start to tremble. "What is this?"

"This is a portrait of our victim. It was generated based on her DNA and refined by using her skeletal features. We believe she was between eighteen months and two years old and may have been dead as long as two years."

"That's really sad but what does it have to do with Nick and me?"

"As I said, there is a familial match between Baby Jane Doe and Nick. He has been excluded as the source of her DNA."

"That doesn't mean she's my kid!" Milo protests.

"That's why we'd like to collect a DNA sample. It would rule you out for certain."

Milo crosses his arms in front of his body and glares at Dakota. "Just how reliable are these DNA tests? I think I remember hearing something about them being challenged in court."

Something about Milo's question strikes me as odd and his body language isn't sitting right with me.

I narrow my gaze and confront him. "Maybe I asked the wrong question. Did you ever father a child with anyone?"

"I don't think so," Milo answers defensively.

"What do you mean? Don't you know?"

"Yes, I know," Milo angerly asserts. After a few beats he admits, "Or maybe not…I guess it's possible."

I snatch the picture out of my brother's hands and point at it. "Are you telling me this is my niece? What did you do to her?"

Milo puts his hands up in front of his chest in a gesture of innocence. "Nothing! I swear. I don't even know if she really is my daughter. I'm just saying it might be possible."

"How?" Dakota asks.

My brother looks down at the camper floor and doesn't meet her eyes as he mumbles, "I stepped out on my wife."

I feel like Milo slapped me. "What do you mean you stepped out on Shalonda? The two of you were two peas in a pod."

Milo leans back against the camper cushions and rests his head against the window. "A lot has changed since you last saw me. You know Shalonda and I went through all the infertility treatments? After we failed three times and ran out of money, Shalonda withdrew and became a totally different person. She started taking far too much prescription medication. I didn't even know who she was anymore. So, I found someone who appreciated me."

"So you had a child with this woman?" Dakota presses.

"This is a long story, but after I started the affair, I started feeling guilty, so I told this woman we couldn't be together anymore because I didn't plan to leave my wife."

"Well, at least you finally came to your senses," I mutter under my breath.

"Yeah, I'm not proud of what I did. So, anyway after I broke it off, my 'friend' told me she was pregnant. I didn't believe her. I thought she was just saying that to keep me around and to destroy my marriage."

I shake my head in dismay. "So you were sleeping around on your wife without protection?"

Milo drags the heels of his hands against his eyes. "What can I say? I was stupid. She said she was clean. She even showed me paperwork and then she told me her tubes were tied."

"What would Mom say if she knew all this?" I spit. It's nearly impossible for me to disguise my disgust.

Milo looks up at me with an expression of horror on his face. "You're not going to tell her, are you? She would hate me forever."

Dakota raises her hand.

Milo and I look at her and in unison ask, "What?"

Dakota clears her throat nervously. "I just want to point out that before you decide to implode your relationship with Thea, you might want to actually do a DNA test to figure out whether Baby Jane Doe is your child."

Milo flinches. "I suppose you're right. What if I am her father? Does that mean I'm going to be charged with her murder? I swear to you, I had nothing to do with that. Until you guys came to talk to me, I had no idea she even existed."

"I can't tell you what law enforcement might choose to do with the information because I'm just a researcher. The easiest way to find out whether you are involved in this case at all is to perform a DNA test to exclude you if you are not Baby Jane Doe's father."

I slam my pop bottle on the table with more force than

I intend and it starts to leak. "Come on Milo. For once in your life, do the right thing. If we are this little girl's family, we have an obligation to find out what happened to her. Right now, they don't even know who she is! We can help this little girl reclaim her identity."

"I can't believe I'm saying this, but okay, I'll get tested. Just tell me what I need to do."

Dakota digs around in her large oversized purse and pulls out a swab and a plastic container. "I need you to rub this around on the inside of your cheek. After you're done, I'll overnight it to our DNA laboratory."

"How long will it take before I know the answer?" Milo asks as he takes the swab from Dakota and rubs the inside of his cheek.

"I'll expedite it as much as I can, but I'm only one DNA specialist in a whole company of specialists, they may have a backlog of tests to process."

"I just can't understand how I could have a child out there and not know it until she's already dead." Milo looks down at his sports watch. "I gotta go back to work." He looks over at me. "You know, you can come visit me even if you're not bringing tragic news."

I stand up and give my brother a one armed hug. "I'll see what I can do. My job keeps me pretty busy. We'll be in touch as soon as the results are available. Thank you for helping us solve the mystery."

Dakota watches me pace around our suite with a look of growing concern. "What's wrong? I thought today went about as well as could be expected. I've had other cases where I was thrown out of the room for confronting someone with DNA results."

I flop down in one of the side chairs. "I'm just so disappointed! My brother isn't who I thought he was. Shalonda was never my favorite person. I wouldn't have chosen her for my brother, but he did. So, if he made those vows, he should've stuck with them."

Unable to sit still, I stand to pace the room again. "I used to worship the ground he walked on. He deserved it too. He often protected me from my father's alcoholic rages and he would purposely let my dad beat on him rather than subject my mom to further harm. So, what is a guy like that doing sleeping around on his wife?"

"I don't have any answers for you other than people change and stress makes you do strange things. I don't have any kids of my own, but my roommate in college had a terrible time getting pregnant. She went through all these fertility treatments and she said the hormones made her feel crazy. You never know, maybe Shalonda was going through something like that."

"All the more reason for my brother not to be a jerk. I guess he's more like my father than I thought. My dad used to do that kind of garbage to my mom. I thought Milo knew better."

"I know what it's like to be disappointed in the people you love. It's an awful feeling. I used to think my dad hung the moon and stars. He bought me a pony for my birthday. I thought he was the best dad ever, right up until he tried to kill my whole entire family." Dakota starts to tear up and angrily wipes away her tears. "I can't believe it's been this many years. I feel as if I'm just as upset about it as I was the day it happened."

I walk over and give her a hug. "I can't imagine."

She buries her face in my chest. "I hate my dad for what he did to all of us. Do you know you are the first man I've ever trusted? I mean, I dated in college but I never let anyone get as close to me as you are. In fact, I never even told them the whole story about my burns. I just kept them covered. People would wonder why I was wearing longsleeved shirts and pants in the middle of summer. I never could bring myself to admit the entire story until I met you."

"I can't imagine how betrayed you must've felt."

"Yeah, it was a real double whammy for me. Not only did I find out my dad was a killer, I found out he had a whole other family besides us. He killed them for life insurance money."

"What a creep!"

"Yeah. As confused as I was about finding out I was adopted, it was a big relief to know I wasn't a blood relative. Like you, I was incredibly confused. I had so many happy memories with the man I thought was my father. To this day, I can't reconcile those with the murderer he actually was. In my head, my father is a convicted murderer but in my heart, he's the guy who taught me how to make chocolate chip pancakes."

I massage Dakota's shoulders with my thumbs. "I see what you did there. I can still love Milo as my brother, but hate his choices."

Dakota wraps her arms around my back and hugs me tightly. "Sometimes, that's the compromise you must make to save your sanity."

"I can't believe you talked me into this. Really? You want to go see a Disney cartoon? No blowing things up or fighting for world dominance?" I ask as I hold Dakota's hand.

She shakes her head. "No, silly! That's the whole point of going to see a kid's movie. We're going to pretend the real world doesn't exist."

"I'll feel stupid. We don't have any kids with us." I look up in the rearview mirror and see the same old blue Cadillac following us. I noticed it a few miles ago.

Abruptly, I turn off the street to see if he follows.

"It doesn't matter. Nobody cares if you take kids to Disney movies."

I glance over at her blankly. I wasn't paying attention to what she said because I'm watching the car follow us turn for turn. "What?"

"I said no one's going to judge you for not bringing kids to a Disney movie. People do it all the time. You think Disneyland is only for kids?"

I make one more turn and the old blue car appears again. The hair on the back of my neck is standing up.

"Where are we going?" Dakota looks out the window.

"This isn't the way to the theater, is it?"

I feign a yawn. "This week has really taken a toll on me. Do you mind if we just rent a movie and go back to the Sweetwater?"

Dakota's brow creases with concern. "Oh, of course. I was looking forward to movie popcorn and hearing other people react to the movie, but I'll live. You seem stressed, is everything okay?"

"It will be when I can hold you safely in my arms," I admit.

Dakota shrugs. "Okay, I was just suggesting a Disney cartoon. It doesn't seem all that dangerous. But whatever floats your boat."

# CHAPTER FIFTEEN

# DAKOTA

I stretch my arms and yawn. The crazy, whirlwind trip to Tennessee has finally caught up with me. I am exhausted to the bone. Again, I'm reminded why I should have kept my emotional distance from Nick. It's far too late now. Anytime I'm not thinking about the case of Baby Jane Doe, I worry about how it's all impacting Nick. All of this stress is making it difficult for me to sleep. It must be the same for Nick. He fell asleep while we were watching Disney movies yesterday. I didn't have the heart to wake him up. He woke up about two in the morning and went back to his room. If he's anything like me, he's probably still sleeping.

I'm relieved to be back home at the Sweetwater. It's funny how quickly this bed-and-breakfast has become my safe place in the world. I snuggle back down into the pillows. The only thing that could make this place better would be if Mr. Pawsome was here with me. Although, I'm sure my mother is spoiling my cat beyond belief.

Just as my eyes are drifting closed, my phone rings with the ring tone I assigned to my mom after my last debacle with her.

"Hi Mom," I answer, trying to force myself to sound as if I've been awake for hours. My mom disapproves of sleeping in for any reason. As a photographer, she loves to catch the sunrise.

"What are you doing?" she abruptly asks.

"I just got home from a grueling business trip. I was trying to catch up on my sleep," I blurt, despite my best intentions.

"You know what I always say … The early bird always gets the best pictures."

"Yeah, I don't think that applies to my life right now."

"How is your case going? Are you going to be able to come home for my birthday after all?"

"The Cold Case Squadron is still gathering data. We're waiting for a key DNA test to come back before we can move the case forward."

"How is it working for all those law enforcement types? Do you have anyone on your team like Derek Morgan from *Criminal Minds*?"

I choke back a laugh. "Mom! Are you lusting after men on television again?"

"What can I say? I'm an artist. I appreciate beauty. The men on that show are positively beautiful!"

Mentally, I review all the members of the Cold Case Squadron. Admittedly, they're all very handsome. Even Pauline is captivating. "Okay, I hate to admit it, but looking at my coworkers at the moment is not  terrible."

"Aha! There's someone you like, I can tell."

Trying to dodge the subject, I ask, "Can I ask you about Dad?"

I hear my mom draw in a deep breath. "You can ask, I don't know if I'll have anything positive to say about the man."

"I know this sounds weird, but I'm just trying to figure out how a guy like him snared someone as smart as you."

My mom heaves a deep sigh. "If I had known the way it was all going to end, I would've never given Sheldon Harper a second glance."

"What was he like in the beginning?"

"Sheldon Harper was everything I wasn't. My family thought of me as just a flighty artist. They were even more critical after I decided to adopt you while I was still single."

"Wait! What? You weren't married to dad when you adopted me? I've never heard the story."

"Oh my goodness! I thought you knew all of this. I'm sorry. We hid the truth from everyone for so long I forgot who knows the truth. You know, this was a time before open adoptions were a thing. I had a friend in our school who was about to be chosen for prestigious apprenticeship. She was horrified to learn she was pregnant. She knew she couldn't afford a baby because her apprenticeship was not paid. Her parents were supporting her and she was sure if they knew she was pregnant they would stop helping her pursue her dreams."

"You know my birth mother?" My voice breaks from the shock.

"Why, yes honey. I did."

"Where is she now?" I demand.

"Nadia tragically passed away from breast cancer about the same time as the house fire."

I practically drop the phone. "Mom! Don't you think

this is something I should have known? Every medical form I've ever filled out asks me about my parents. This is important information."

"You'd already been through so much, I didn't want to add more tragedy than you'd already suffered. After all, you were such a little survivor already."

"Okay, I guess you can't go back and change it now. But it would've been nice to know. So, how does Sheldon Harper play into all this?"

"So, I went into the mortgage company to see if I could pull out some equity to pay for your adoption. Sheldon Harper was so handsome and he genuinely seemed to care for me and my struggles. He helped me pay my bills and rearranged my house financing so I was paying less even though I had pulled out money for your adoption. After everything was all done, Sheldon asked to go out with me. At first, I told him no because I was too busy with you."

"I wish you would've stuck with that answer," I mutter under my breath.

"Me too, honey. Me too! But I didn't stay away even though my life was crazy. When you were little, I was busy working at one of those cheesy glamour shot places. I took you over to my sister's house when I was working and the hours were insanely long. Sheldon Harper came riding in like a knight on a white horse. He promised that he could take care of us. I believed him. He had a dependable job where he got lots of respect as a mortgage broker. I didn't know he had a whole other identity."

"Mom, do you think you could have chosen not to fall in love with him?"

"What kind of question is that?"

"An honest one. There is a guy here in Florida. I like him very much. But getting together with him right now would be a really, really bad idea. Yet, I can't stop thinking about him."

"Oh, honey. Just watch yourself. I don't want history to repeat itself. You should have better taste in men than me because mine was about as awful as it comes."

"Mom, dad has been in jail for a really long time. How come you haven't found love with someone else?"

"I wish I could. But I don't trust myself to make the right call after what happened with your father. So, it's better for me to be alone than to choose someone only to find out that they are a killer or child abuser or something like that."

"Oh man! I had no idea you had the same issues with trust as me."

"It's too late for me now, but you are still young. You should learn to trust your heart. Don't lose hope because that's all we have."

I smile even though my mom can't see me. "Is that why my middle name is Hope?"

"You were the best thing that ever happened to me. You were my hope for a new, happy life."

Dylan sets a piece of paper down in front of me. As he does so, he puts his hand on my shoulder. "The results of the DNA tests are back. I'm not sure they are exactly what you wanted them to be."

The blood drains from my face. Honestly, I don't know

what I was hoping for either. But Dylan's expression tells me the story. I don't even have to look at the report.

Steeling myself, I pick up the paper and confirm my worst suspicions. My eyes tear up as I read that Milo Galeon Weston is a 99.3 percent match to Baby Jane Doe.

A wave of panic overtakes me as I look up at Dylan. "This is going to kill him, you know that right?" I pause as I try to collect myself. "This is going to destroy any hope of us," I add in a soft whisper.

"Not necessarily," Dylan assures me.

"How can this be anything but the end of my relationship with Nick? Even though I didn't cause this to happen, he's going to blame me for bringing turmoil to his family life."

"Do you know the story of how my fiancé, Lauren and I met?"

"Ketki told me you guys met on a case."

Dylan nods solemnly. "Not just any case. I went searching for Lauren's sister during my first mission as commander of the Cold Case Squadron."

"How sweet!"

"Not so sweet. I discovered that April had been killed. Not only that, Lauren's mother played a role in introducing the killer to her daughter. As you can imagine, that made things dicey between us for a while."

"Wow! Then you really do know what I'm going through. I just don't know what to do. Anything I do is going to break his heart."

"Do you believe Nick is involved in the death of Baby Jane Doe? Is he covering for his brother?"

I shake my head vehemently. "It doesn't seem like it.

He was furious that there was a possibility his brother could be the father of this poor little baby. When we first met, he was completely blindsided by what I was telling him."

"So, if you believe him, then you have to decide how to proceed in a way that doesn't harm the case against Baby Jane Doe's killer — but still allows you and Nick to be happy."

"It's that last part that I struggle with."

Dylan pats me on the shoulder. "Trust me, I understand. I also know that if your relationship is worth saving, the timing issues can be solved."

I dab away tears. "Thank you so much. That makes me feel so much better."

"Hang in there and try to find some hope."

My stomach is in knots by the time I get to the Sweetwater. I tried to call Nick from the office but Tristan returned my call. Apparently, Identity Bank is dealing with a top-secret issue which he couldn't discuss and he wanted to let me know Nick may not be available for a few hours.

In an effort to kill time, I try to relax in the Jacuzzi tub in my room. Usually, the jets would be enough to soothe me. Tonight, they seem more annoying than helpful.

My phone vibrates against the edge of the tub. It startles me so much I almost drop my phone into the water.

"Hello?" I answer as I try to catch my breath.

"Dakota, this is Nick. Tristan said you called."

"I did. I didn't realize you were in the field today."

"Yeah, we were tasked with protecting a high level diplomat. We didn't have any notice or I would've let you know."

"That's all right. I wasn't keeping tabs on you. I just need to talk to you."

"We can do that. I've had a long day. Where do you want to meet?"

"It's been a long day for me too. Can you meet me at the Sweetwater?"

"Okay, I'll be there in a few minutes. Seeing you will be the highlight of my day."

I struggle with the temptation to blurt out the whole story and just get it over with. Instead, I say, "Looking forward to it." That may be the biggest fib I've ever told in my life. I am so not looking forward to this conversation.

# Chapter Sixteen

# Nick

If I'd been paying more attention to Dakota's request, I probably would've been more prepared for the expression on her face when she answered the door.

Dakota looks very much on the verge of tears as she swings the door open. Wordlessly, she takes the pizza and soda from my hands and sets them on the table. Her stomach audibly growls when she smells the pizza. This is not the first time we've done this routine. We discovered we both have a taste for exotic pizza. So, tonight's fare is chicken artichoke pizza with spinach and tomatoes.

Usually, such a gift is rewarded with enthusiasm. Sadly, no hugs and smiles are present tonight.

I sigh and sit down at the little table in the kitchenette. "You might as well not beat around the bush. I can tell you have bad news. So, I have to ask — my mother or my brother?"

Dakota swallows hard. "I'm so sorry. The DNA results came back today and your brother is indeed the father of Baby Jane Doe."

"This is a freaking nightmare. I mean, I knew it was a

possibility because of the work you've done with Toby and Phoenix. It's hard to refute that picture. Even so, I was hoping against hope it was not accurate."

Dakota bristles. "I tried to tell you we don't pull this stuff out of the sky. There is real science behind my work. I'm sorry it turned out to be your brother. Please remember, I'm only the messenger."

"I didn't mean it that way. I meant it in the sense that I was praying for a miracle. More than anything else, I don't want my brother to be wrapped up in all of this. My mother will be absolutely crushed. She complains all the time that Milo and I haven't given her any grandchildren. Now, on the day she finds out she had a grandchild, she also knows her grandbaby is dead. There is no way to make that okay."

"You're right. This is going to be awful anyway you look at it."

"You want to come with me so we can get some answers from Milo?"

"Are you sure? I am the person who represents everything horrible that's about to happen to him."

"Yes I'm sure. I need you there so I'm not tempted to beat that dirty, rotten gigolo."

Dakota lets loose with a startled laugh. "Did you just call your brother a gigolo? I don't think you have facts in evidence to support that conclusion."

"I'm only calling him that so I don't call him something much worse. Let's go talk to him and figure out what's going on."

I start to stalk out of the room. Dakota runs behind me and places her hand on my forearm to stop me. "I think we need a plan unless you want to walk all the way to Tennessee."

I dig my phone out of my pocket and hold it up in the air. "Well then, I guess it's a really good thing I have Tristan on speed dial. Although, right now I'm so mad at my brother I could probably walk to Tennessee faster than we can arrange a flight."

Fortunately for my big brother, today is Saturday and he isn't working. It's a good thing for him that Dakota is with me. Otherwise, I might be tempted to beat the snot out of him even though he's bigger than me.

Milo is surprised to find us standing in front of his trailer. I don't blame him.

When he recovers from the surprise of our presence, he quips, "So, I guess the test was positive and I'm the match?"

"This is no joking matter, Milo. A child is dead. *Your* child is dead. Nothing much funny about that. So, we need to talk to you about what you know about Baby Jane Doe."

"Okay, come on in," he says as he steps away from the door.

I look around the small apartment. "Where is Shalonda?"

My brother hangs his head. "Shalonda and I haven't been together in a few years. She just couldn't get over my affair. It's ironic, she didn't have any idea I had a child. She was just pissed that I wasn't faithful."

"Imagine that," Dakota mutters quietly.

"Sorry, I wasn't trying to suggest she shouldn't be upset. I'm just telling you why she's not here. I blew it with her."

After we arrange ourselves in the living room, I scoot the sheet of paper Dakota gave me across the coffee table toward my brother. "If you needed more proof than the picture we showed you last time, there it is. You are Baby Jane Doe's father. You need to level with us and tell us everything you know."

Milo glances down at the floor. "I told you everything I know about her. I thought she was a figment of imagination of someone who was trying to manipulate me. I never for a moment believed I had a child out in the world. After all, Shalonda and I had been trying to create one for more than half a decade. How was I supposed to know my stupidity would create a child?"

"I know Mom gave you the lecture about what causes these things because you gave it to me."

Milo takes off his glasses and pinches the bridge of his nose. "You're a funny guy, but that's not real helpful now. What happened is over and done with. We just have to figure out what to do from here."

Dakota takes a small pad of paper and pen out of her purse. She glances up expectantly. "What can you tell me about your child's mother? We'll need to track her down and perform a DNA test to confirm your allegations."

My brother looks like he would rather go to the dentist then answer her question — and after several years of orthodontia, he absolutely loathes going to the dentist. He averts his gaze. "I'd rather not drag her into all this. We were together a long time ago. What's between us is ancient history."

"I don't think you understand the implications of all of this. Someone killed your daughter, Milo. If that person wasn't you, you need to let law enforcement know everything — even if it's embarrassing. You don't have the luxury of ignoring the facts in this case."

My stomach lurches as the ramifications of Dakota's warning sinks in.

"Darn it, Milo! Don't make a terrible situation worse. This isn't the time to care about your ego. Your daughter has been murdered! That should mean something to you. It scares me that you don't even seem to care."

Milo stands up and sticks his finger in my face. "No! I do care. You've got this all wrong. I'm not protecting my child's mother, I'm protecting everyone else I love."

I push right back. "What in the heck does that even mean? How does not disclosing who it is protect your family? Whoever it is could be a murderer for all we know. So, you might as well tell us."

Milo looks unsteady on his feet before he whispers, "I just can't."

I give him a hard look. "Can't? Or won't? Either way, it's an idiotic decision which could land you in the crosshairs of the police or the FBI. I can't believe you are being so stubborn."

"If I tell you, it will destroy you, mom and even grandma. I'd almost rather be falsely accused of killing my daughter than hurt all of you."

My blood is pounding in my ears. I've been angry at my brother more times than I care to count, but I've never been more pissed off than I am at this moment.

Out of the corner of my eye, I see Dakota gasp and cover her mouth. I spin around to face her. "What?"

"I think I've figured out why your brother doesn't want

to tell you who Baby Jane Doe's mother is."

"Oh, man! This is a nightmare," Milo mutters under his breath.

With a sinking feeling, I ask, "Dakota, what is Milo hiding from me?"

Dakota nervously plays with her long blonde hair. "I don't know this to a one hundred percent scientific certainty, but if I was to venture a guess I'd say the mother of his child is Cheryl."

"Cheryl Scroggins?" I clarify as I try to absorb what she just revealed. "Is Dakota right?" I demand.

Milo hangs his head. "Yes." His response is so quiet, I can barely hear it.

In the next second, I simply react to my white-hot rage. My fist connects with his cheekbone with lightning fast speed and a considerable amount of force.

He stumbles back as Dakota gasps in shock.

Milo stands up and rubs his cheek. "I deserve that. I see you haven't lost your hand-to-hand combat skills."

"Darn straight. What in the heck were you thinking? Cheryl and I have been practically engaged since we were in junior high school. Why would you do that to me?"

"I don't know. I told you it was the most idiotic decision of my entire life. I'd like to tell you my choices didn't have anything to do with you, but that's not exactly true."

I clench my fists at my sides. I am sorely tempted to pummel him beyond recognition. But, I am not my father.

Dakota seems to recognize my struggle. She places her hand on my forearm. I unclench my fist and intertwine my fingers with hers. I blow out a deep breath.

"You might want to explain your statement to your brother before he decides to deck you again," Dakota replies as she squeezes my hand.

"Yeah, I'd like to make your pretty face not so pretty right now. So, you better tell me what you mean."

Milo rakes his hand through his hair. "Look, I know this makes me sound pathetic — but I've always been jealous of you."

"Jealous of me? Why? You're taller, stronger and smarter."

Milo smirks. "All evidence to the contrary. If I was smarter than you, we wouldn't be having this conversation. Anyway, you always seemed to have everything I wanted. You and Cheryl got together before I even had a girlfriend and you always seemed to be able to work through whatever. Then, you got into the military and they excluded me because of my sickle-cell anemia. Even after you were injured in the military you landed a cushy job as a bodyguard for the rich and famous. I just never had that kind of luck. So, when my marriage was disintegrating and Cheryl came on to me, it seemed like a way to get something you couldn't have for once."

I do some mental math and it dawns on me my brother was sleeping with the person I thought was going to marry me during the time I was overseas serving in the sandbox.

"You're an extra special jerk! You slept with my girlfriend while I was deployed, didn't you?"

Milo nods. "I'm so sorry. It was the biggest mistake of my life. It ruined everything I had going for me."

I turn to Dakota and flash her a brief smile. "Lucky for you, I don't care about Cheryl anymore. I have found more happiness with Dakota in just a few short weeks than

I had in more than a decade and a half with Cheryl. So while it might be awkward between us for a while, you have a bigger issue."

"Yeah? What's bigger than this?"

Dakota sighs. "You better pray the mother of your child is not also her killer."

# CHAPTER SEVENTEEN

# DAKOTA

If there is one place I never thought I would be, it's holding a shaking man in the middle of a bed with linen bed coverings while sitting on a private plane waiting for a mechanic to perform an emergency repair before we take off.

Yet, here I am. As frightening as it is to see such a strong fighter falling apart in my arms, there's no place on the planet I would rather be.

Intellectually, I know I should be keeping my distance and professional objectivity. Somehow, that idea has flown out the window. I've always been a helper. Nick needs all the help he can get right now.

I shift on the bed as I try to relieve a pinched nerve in my shoulder. The movement makes Nick stir.

He straightens out his T-shirt as he sits up. "You must think I'm a blubbering idiot. I can't believe this hit me so hard."

I run my fingers through his hair. "Don't worry about it. When your body dumps a ton of adrenaline, there's not much you can do about it. When you add that on top of extreme sadness and disappointment, it's no surprise you crashed and burned for a bit."

Nick shrugs. "I'm a former military pilot, I should have a better handle on things."

The corner of my mouth hitches up. "Handling your work life and personal business are two different skills. Trust me, if they weren't, I wouldn't be here with you."

Nick sits a little straighter and looks me straight in the eyes. "If being together with me jeopardizes your career, you have to let me know. I don't want you to pay the price for my brother's stupid mistakes."

I roll my shoulder with what I hope is nonchalance as I confess, "It's not as if I've made a secret of how I feel about you. In fact, Dylan and I discussed it the other day."

Nick stiffens. "Yeah … How did that go?"

"Remarkably well. I was worried the DNA results would spell the end of us. Dylan was very encouraging that we could weather the storm."

I feel Nick relax against me. "That's good to hear. Did he have anything else to say?"

"He said we've probably pursued this case as far as we can on our own. We need to start involving other members of the Cold Case Squadron to help ensure the case has integrity when it goes to court."

"I presume he said all of this before we discovered my former girlfriend is Baby Jane Doe's mother?"

I nod. "Yes, I imagine he'd tell me that it's even more important to stay above the fray."

Nick chuckles. "Above the fray. Yeah … Right. I'm totally in the fray. You know, all this time I thought Cheryl was keeping her distance because she hated the fact that I was in the military. Now I find out the real reason is because she was sleeping with my brother. I feel like a massive idiot."

I take a moment to hug Nick. "You are not the idiot in the situation. You were serving your country. The fact that she decided to stray has nothing to do with who you are or whether you failed at your relationship."

Nick cringes. "Yeah, that's nice of you to say. But she slept with Milo. Of all the people on the planet, she had to choose my brother?"

"I'm not accusing her of being the brightest bulb in the bunch. I'm just saying it's not your fault. You shouldn't have had to choose between a happy relationship and your military service. If she really loved you, she would have supported you no matter what. So, I guess what I'm saying is you dodged a  huge bullet."

Nick lets out a surprised burst of laughter. "Are you telling me to count my blessings because if things would've gone differently I would've been married to a manipulative, sociopathic witch?"

I grin. "Pretty much. I might be shy and awkward, but you're better off with me. I would never, I mean *ever* sleep with your brother."

Nick looks horrified. "I should hope not! At the moment, Milo is not my favorite person." He leans over to kiss me thoroughly. "However, you are without a doubt allowed in my life for as long as you want to be here."

I snuggle against his chest and drop a kiss on the hollow of his neck. "We may not have met under ideal circumstances, but there's nowhere else I'd rather be than beside you."

Nick rubs my shoulder. "So, what's next? I'm not

willing to lose you over Milo and Cheryl's stupidity. I'd like to find out who my niece was and hold someone responsible for her death."

"I think we follow directions. Dylan was very clear that it's time to bring in the rest of the team. I know I want to hear from Cheryl. If we're looking for answers, she is the logical place to start."

Nick sits up and moves away from me. "I hope you don't mind, I'm going to skip that interrogation. If I was angry enough to punch my brother, there's no telling what I might do to Cheryl. That woman owned me heart and soul. She chose to rip out my heart and stomp on it. Honestly, I have no desire to ever see her again unless her butt is hauled in front of the judge and she's sentenced to a good long prison term."

My eyes widen. "Well then ... I guess I don't have to worry about you wanting to get back together with your ex."

"Nah, at one point I was really broken up over the fact that she married someone else. Now, I would just as soon she burn in hell if she had anything to do with Baby Jane Doe's death."

"I'll do my best to figure out what happened to your niece. I'm just worried your brother has more involvement than he's admitting to."

Nick sighs. "If that's true, he can join Cheryl in purgatory, for all I care."

I scroll through the electronic file Toby created for me as Pauline drives to Cheryl's house.

"I don't know how helpful I'm going to be. I pretty much hate Cheryl Scroggins by definition because she hurt Nick. I won't be real big on objectivity."

Pauline giggles. "Oh, I hear you. Just do what I do if I've heard of the suspect or interacted with them before. I ask myself if I would be asking them this particular question if I didn't know about them in advance. If the answer is no, I have to decide why I am really pursuing a line of questioning. This helps me try to leave my prejudices outside the interrogation room door."

"Prejudice is a light word for what I'm feeling. I don't know if I can set my feelings about her aside."

"Notice I said try to. Sometimes, I'm not always successful. Just try to remember your overarching purpose. You are pursuing this case to get justice for Baby Jane Doe and find out who she is and why she died. If you focus on that, it'll be much easier to set aside your personal feelings."

We pull up to a nice house in a quiet neighborhood.

After Pauline double-checks the address, she says to me, "Are you ready to find justice for Baby Jane Doe?"

I shrug. "About ready as I'll ever be. Hopefully Cheryl has some answers."

When Pauline knocks on the front door, a tall, thin woman with high cheekbones and beautiful long hair as black as a raven wing answers the door. "Are you Cheryl Scroggins?"

The woman flashes a large diamond ring in front of Pauline's face. "Not anymore. I'm Cheryl Long now. Who's asking?"

I step forward and extend my hand for her to shake. "Good morning. I'm Dr. Dakota Crenshaw. This is my colleague on the Cold Case Squadron, Pauline Lawrence-

Payne."

"What do you want? If you're here to convince me to go to your church, I already have a church home. I go with my husband, Bubba."

Pauline grins. "Oh good! I'm glad I'm not the only person annoyed by door-to-door solicitors. Anyway, that's not what we're here for. May we come in and explain?"

Cheryl shrugs. "Go ahead, I guess. Bubba is out playing golf, he should be back soon."

"That's all right, we're here to talk to you, actually. It might be easier without him present."

Cheryl opens her door wide and points to the couch. "Have a seat. Sorry the place is messy, I wasn't expecting company."

"Don't worry about it. Your home is beautiful," Pauline remarks.

"Who did you say you work for again?"

I pull out a business card and hand it to Cheryl. "I am a forensic genealogist. I use DNA technology to solve murder cases."

"Murders? I don't know anyone who's been killed."

"That's what we are here to find out, ma'am," Pauline replies.

"You think I killed somebody?" she says as her jaw goes slack. "I never did anything to anyone, why are you really here?"

"To be more specific, we're here to eliminate your DNA," I add.

"I don't understand. I haven't committed a crime. So I have no idea what you're talking about."

Pauline presses her lips together. "Gee, that's too bad. I was hoping to get some answers. See, your name came up in our investigation. I'd like to get a DNA sample to exclude you from consideration. It will make our investigation so much easier."

"Investigation into what?"

"Fitzgerald Forensics was called in to help identify the remains of a missing child and to bring her killer to justice."

Cheryl theatrically covers her chest as she gasps. "What does that have to do with me? As you can see, it's just my husband and me. I haven't killed anyone."

"You may not have killed her, but we have reason to believe you are the mother of the child we are trying to identify. We call her Baby Jane Doe, but that's only because we don't have a name. Our purpose here today is to try to figure out what happened to Baby Jane Doe and give her back her identity."

Cheryl's face tightens. "What does this have to do with me?" she asks in a voice cracking with emotion.

"There's no easy way to sugarcoat this or make it easier to understand. It just is what it is. Pauline and I need to know if you have a daughter between the ages of eighteen months and two years old."

Cheryl sways on her feet as she walks over to her couch and sinks down into the cushions.

She buries her hands in her face. "Are you here to tell me you found Harmony?"

"Harmony?" I parrot.

She nods. "Yeah, my daughter, Harmony Hope," she clarifies as if I should know who she's speaking of."

"How old is your daughter?" Pauline has the presence to ask.

"Last time I saw her, Harmony was twenty months old."

"What do you mean?" I press. "How long has it been since you've seen her?"

"Twenty-six months." Cheryl answers succinctly. "She's been gone longer than I had her now."

A dark feeling of dread fills me. "Where did Harmony Hope go?"

Cheryl shrugs. "I assume her father has her."

Pauline shakes her head. "We've established that Milo Weston doesn't have your daughter. So, how about telling us the truth for a change?"

"What do you mean Milo doesn't have Harmony? I got a note saying he was going to take custody," Cheryl asks as her voice fills with panic.

Pauline pulls out her notebook and holds a pen poised to take notes. "Maybe you should start from the beginning. Are you saying you were in a relationship with Milo Weston?"

Cheryl suddenly becomes interested in a stain on her carpet as she answers, "I was in something with Milo — but calling it a relationship might be a bit much. Look, I never planned to get pregnant. Milo thought he couldn't have kids. So we were just messing around. I was trying to make his brother jealous. Nobody was more shocked than me."

"Are you sure it's Milo's child?" Pauline presses.

Cheryl looks like Pauline slapped her across the face. "Of course I'm sure. Nicholas was overseas playing G.I.

Joe, even though I asked him not to join. So, I thought if I slept with Milo, I would finally get his attention and he would stay home for a change."

I physically have to bite my tongue to stop from blurting out my opinion.

"Okay, so you made some less than optimal choices and had a baby. Why didn't you report her missing?"

Cheryl groans. "If I tell you the truth, you're going to think I am a terrible mother. Go ahead. There's nothing you can say about me that I haven't already said to myself."

"Cheryl, why didn't you report your daughter missing?" Pauline repeats.

"I honestly thought she was with Milo and I figured he would be a better father than I was a mother. After Milo broke it off with me, I got together with this guy I met online. Boy, was that a mistake. He turned out to be a first class jerk. He was beating on me every day. So I figured Harmony would be safer with her dad. When I got that note, I was relieved that she was finally in a safe place. I mean, George told me he wasn't hurting my daughter, but he also told me that the reason he was hitting me was because I made him too mad. I knew that wasn't true. So, I was afraid he was lying about never hurting Harmony."

Pauline and I look at each other with alarm before I ask, "Whatever happened to George? He's not the guy you married is he?"

"Oh good grief! No way! I finally got up enough nerve to tell Milo about Harmony and then I got the heck out of there. George wasn't too happy about that and he beat the crap out of me. My neighbor saw what was happening and called the police. They hauled George off to jail and he got in a knife fight during breakfast. He didn't even live long enough to go to court. It was karma at its finest. I can't tell you how many times George held me at knifepoint and threatened to kill us both."

"Do you believe George could have done something to Harmony?"

"Not as far as I know! I thought she was with Milo. Are you sure she's not? He could be doing all of this to set me up for something I didn't do. Milo was furious at me when I told him I was pregnant. He thought I was just manipulating him. This could be his twisted form of payback."

The corner of Pauline's mouth hitches up. "There are some people in Milo's camp who think you are the one who is capable of harming a child."

"Who would think such a thing? I loved my daughter. I loved her enough to get away from the person who was abusing us. I thought she was safe with her dad. If I didn't, I would've moved heaven and earth to find her."

"I hate to tell you this, but someone murdered your daughter and stuffed her down a well. Right at this moment, you look like our best suspect. No mother I know would give up her daughter without so much as a backward glance. In my mind, this is enough to make you more than just a person of interest."

"I swear to you, after I told Milo about Harmony again, I got a note from him telling me that if I knew what was good for me, I would let him take custody and never fight it in court. Since I was fighting for my own life as I tried to get away from George, I just figured it was the right decision. It doesn't mean I don't miss her every single day of her life."

"You have a funny way of showing it," I mutter under

my breath.

"Okay, judge all you want, but you've never been in my shoes. I had to make incredibly tough decisions. I thought I was making the right one for Harmony. How was I supposed to know something happened to her?"

I now understand Nick's compulsion to punch his brother. "So, you're saying you never contacted Milo and his wife to see how Harmony was doing?"

Cheryl shakes her head. "Oh, no. I met Milo's wife once. I think she knew something was going on between Milo and me. So, I kept my distance. I had enough drama going on in my life, I didn't need any more."

Pauline frowns. "So, I just want to make sure I got the facts straight. You had a baby and you didn't tell Mr. Weston. You raised that baby for almost two years, loving and caring for her every second of the way, but when she disappears from your life and stays gone for more than two years, you don't even tell anybody?"

"That's what I'm saying!" Cheryl shoots back.

"What about your family? Didn't they suspect something was wrong when your daughter was missing?"

Cheryl hangs her head. "I told my family I met some rich rap star who didn't want to be public about our relationship. My grandma is really good friends with Milo's family. I didn't want to bring shame on her. So, they all think some rich music mogul won custody of Harmony."

Pauline sighs and closes her notebook. "For the record, I don't believe you. You're going to have to do a lot to prove that your story is credible. I think the first step is for you to provide us with a DNA sample so that we can definitively prove you are the mother of the baby we know as Baby Jane Doe. After those results come back, if you are her mother, you are going to have to give a minute by minute account of how your daughter disappeared without you raising any alarm bells to anyone."

"Let's just say I don't believe you either," Cheryl challenges. "Maybe you've just made this whole thing up. I bet Harmony Hope is just fine somewhere and Milo wants to sue me for child support or something."

"Are you sure you want proof of what happened to your daughter?" I ask. "Be careful what you ask for."

Cheryl crosses her arms in front of her. "If you got it, flaunt it," she challenges in a dismissive voice.

I pull the pictures out of the file and hold them in front of her. "The first picture is of your daughter's bones we pulled from the well. The second picture is generated based on her genetic genome. We anticipate this is what your daughter would look like if she were alive."

Cheryl snatches the pictures from my hand to get a closer look. When she does, she turns pale. "Oh my gosh! That's my baby. They even got the little space between her teeth. It looks just like her!"

Pauline leans forward. "So, Cheryl, let me spell it out for you. If this is your daughter, someone killed her and dumped her in the bottom of an abandoned well. If you did not murder her, you need to help us find who did. Are you ready to take a DNA test?"

Tears flow down Cheryl's face. It's as if the full impact of what we've been saying the whole time has just now hit. "Oh, my poor baby! Who would do this to you?"

I dig in my purse and remove a DNA collection kit. "We don't know. We need to take your DNA to confirm Baby Jane Doe is Harmony Hope. If she is, we'll need your assistance. You knew her better than any person on the planet. So, we're counting on you to do the right thing."

"Of course, you can take all the DNA you want. That little girl was mine and something horrible happened to her. It wasn't me, so someone else needs to pay."

I look her in the eye as I promise, "I started this case to make sure Baby Jane Doe could find her identity and her way back to her family. If you've got something to tell us, now is the time."

Cheryl holds up her hands in a gesture of innocence. "I swear, I've told you everything I know. I thought Milo had taken her and made her part of his perfect little family. If I had any idea something bad had happened to Harmony, you better believe I would have been shouting from the rooftops."

Pauline stands and gathers her belongings. "Like I said, you are my primary suspect. If the evidence proves me wrong, I sincerely apologize. But you had every reason to get rid of your child. You started a new relationship and you were unable to get back together with your daughter's father. More than one mother has murdered her child in the name of improving their love life. Who's to say that's not what you did?"

"I swear I didn't," Cheryl asserts as she crosses her chest in front of her.

Pauline nods tightly. "You'd be surprised how many people say that too. We'll see if the evidence supports the truth as you see it."

# CHAPTER EIGHTEEN

# NICK

Dakota screeches in delight when she sees her cat, Mr. Pawsome.

"Oh my gosh! This is the best welcome home present ever! How did he get here?"

I shrug. "It's a long story. Apparently, you gave your mom my number as an emergency contact while you were out of town. Your mom got curious and reached out to me. When I explained why I was here instead of with you, she offered to let me babysit your cat for you so that you would feel loved and at home."

"How did he get here from Virginia?" I ask. My voice squeaks at the end.

Mr. Pawsome purrs when I scratch his ears. "Well, Tristan may have provided a lift on his private plane."

"You flew to Virginia on a private plane to go pick up my cat? You all are insane. You are incredibly sweet, but —"

Mr. Pawsome jumps from my arms to Dakota's shoulder. He starts to play with her dangling earrings. "Oh my gosh! I missed him so much. But I can't believe you went to all this work for me."

I shrug. "You know Tristan, he's all about reuniting families. Speaking of reuniting families, how did it go with Cheryl?"

Dakota clears her throat. "I can see why you were in love with her for so long. She is incredibly attractive."

I scoff. "She may be beautiful on the outside, but she is ugly to the core on the inside. If she wasn't, she would have never betrayed me by sleeping with Milo."

"She didn't have any trouble admitting that she had slept with your brother. She told me that she did it to make you jealous. She thought you would abandon your military career to save your relationship."

"The ironic thing is if she had waited a few more months, a terrorist IED took me out instead. She could have had everything she wanted if she would've just been patient."

"I wasn't expecting to like her at all, but I get the feeling she regrets everything that happened between her and Milo."

I suck in a breath as I absorb her words. "Too little, too late. So, did she admit that Baby Jane Doe is her daughter?"

Dakota nods. "Yes, she even agreed to a DNA test so we can establish maternity."

"Oh, so she didn't admit Baby Jane Doe is hers? She is making you prove it with a DNA test? Isn't Milo's word good enough?"

"She didn't deny Baby Jane Doe is hers. She didn't even try to claim that Milo wasn't the father. We just need to make sure the case is rock solid."

"What did she tell you happened to my niece?"

"Apparently, she thought your brother had taken custody of his daughter."

"How could he do that?" I bellow. "He didn't even know the baby existed until after she was dead."

I nod. "I understand that. Your niece's name was Harmony Hope. No wonder I felt so connected to her. We share the same middle name."

I shut my eyes and rub my temple. "It would have been nice if she chose to tell my family about her daughter before Harmony was murdered, don't you think?"

I nod. "Finding out the truth too late can be really destructive."

"So, she's claiming she never hurt Harmony even though she was presumably the last person to see her?"

"Yeah, she's claiming she thought Milo and Shalonda had Harmony all this time."

I shake my head in disgust. "No wonder we couldn't make it as a couple. She's even more delusional than I remember."

Dakota presses her lips together. "It's not my story to tell, but it's possible Cheryl had extenuating circumstances."

"Did she report Harmony missing? No! I don't think she did. Otherwise, you would've found out my niece's identity long before you had to revert to using complicated DNA testing. Knowing Cheryl, she probably killed her daughter to get attention from people."

"Oh wow! A little harsh, aren't you? You don't know what she was going through when all this went down."

"With all due respect, neither do you. All I know about

my ex-girlfriend is that she is the queen of manipulation. If she hadn't been, I'd still be with her and the next wedding would've been mine instead of Dylan's."

Dakota digs through her purse and pulls out the cream-colored invitation. "Speaking of weddings, Dylan invited me to his. I couldn't believe it, I barely know him. He wrote me a note telling me he wanted me to come so that I could see that real love can grow in the middle of chaos and bring happiness."

"Hmm, I wonder if Dylan is playing the role of matchmaker. He sent me an invitation too. He wanted me to make sure that I was available to escort you and keep you safe."

"Something tells me Dylan is a bit of a closet romantic."

I chuckle. "Oh, since Dylan met Lauren, there's no disguising his inner romantic. He has it on full display. Since you're going to the wedding anyway, do you want me to tag along for company?"

Dakota smiles. "The last time we crashed a wedding, I had a blast. I would love to go with you."

I take a moment to relish the feeling of Dakota in my arms. "We have too much pain and sadness in our lives right now. We should steal as many moments of happiness as we can find."

This time, I'm not late to the Cold Case Squadron briefing. Even so, I can tell from the look on Dakota's face that any new developments haven't been positive.

She walks by me and pauses to whisper in my ear,

"This is going to be a rough one. Are you sure you want to be here?"

I nod. I don't know if I'll ever be okay with the idea that my former girlfriend had a baby with my brother and may be implicated for a murder. However, given the current situation, I've accepted it as well as I possibly can.

Dylan clears his throat. "Thank you for coming today. Dakota has an update for us which might be difficult for some of you to take." He pauses to look directly at me and Dakota. "If this is too difficult for you to process, you have my permission to leave this briefing."

Dakota looks startled. "Okay … I'm not sure I should leave since I'm the one giving the report."

Dylan glances toward the front of the room. "Look, if this is going to be difficult for you, I can read the report as well as you can."

Dakota's spine stiffens. "I'm confident in my ability to remain objective."

Dylan levels me with a pained gaze. "What about you, Weston?"

I shrug. "I'm not going into this blind. I have a really good idea what those results will show. As difficult as it is for me, they are not going to dissuade me from searching for the truth in this case."

Dylan nods encouragement. "Very well then. Dakota, can you tell this task force what you found?"

Dakota flinches. "Some days, my job is easier than others. Today is a particularly tough day. I'm sorry, Nick. Milo Weston and Cheryl Scroggins are the biological parents of Baby Jane Doe, now known as Harmony Hope."

Cody doesn't even look surprised when he pulls out his ever present pad of paper and pencil. "Okay, now that the mystery is over, are we going to be able to bring these creeps to justice?"

Dakota looks uncomfortable before she admits, "I honestly don't know. They all seem to be standing in a circle and pointing at each other."

Frank raises his hand. "You know what I used to do when I was the agent? If I had subjects who were pointing the finger at each other, I would put them all in the same room for questioning. That way, they don't have the luxury of putting someone else on the hook for something they didn't do. Their claims are pretty much fact checked in real time."

"If you want me to be in the same room as my brother and my ex while I'm calm, cool, and collected, you'll probably have to sedate me."

Pauline writes something on the pad of paper in front of her before she looks up at me. "That's actually a really good idea."

"It is?" I ask, surprise colors my voice.

Pauline nods enthusiastically. "Well, not so much the sedating part ... but I think it would be helpful for you to be in the room when they confront each other. You seem to provoke strong emotions in both of them. So, having you there would increase the chance that they will admit to something they might otherwise keep to themselves. Stress can make everyone talk more than they intend to."

Dakota bites her bottom lip. "I'm not sure that's such a great idea," Dakota cautions. "You are aware that Nick hauled off and hit Milo the last time they were together, right?"

Frank rubs his hands together in anticipation. "That's what makes cases like this interesting. In my experience, family members are far more cruel to each other than they are to strangers." Frank looks directly at me. "You may be just the catalyst we need to get the ball rolling."

Unconsciously, I roll my eyes. "Or, I may be the thing that blows this case apart to the point where it can't be salvaged. Are you sure you want me involved?"

Frank and Dylan nod their heads. "Sometimes, people need to be encouraged to come off the story they originally told. Having you there might encourage both of them to tell the truth."

Tristan clicks his pen. "That settles it. We are going to take the whole Cold Case Squadron to Tennessee and see what we can shake out of the bushes. We've been sitting on this case for too long."

I try again, "Y'all know I'm ticked off at both parties involved, right?"

"Mmm-hmm," Frank says as he smiles. "Sometimes, people who lie need an outside agitator to help them see the truth."

Dylan turns to Tristan. "I guess the team will be flying to Tennessee again so it would be handy to borrow your plane. I have one request. Can we get this done and over with as soon as possible so I can get married and go on a honeymoon?"

Tristan grins. "As you know, cases typically resolve on their own timetable. So, I can't make any guarantees. Then again, I'm all for honeymoons in Paris on a random Tuesday afternoon."

Dylan blanches. "Okay… I'll let you know if I want to take you up on that. Hopefully, everything will fall in place and we can do things the way we planned."

# Chapter Nineteen

# Dakota

"Jamie, I thought you were kidding when you said you wanted to come to Florida to work on this case. Is Dr. Fitzgerald okay with this?"

"If he's not, it's a little late now because I'm here. My trip to Disney World is just an added perk of the job."

"Whatever. It's not like I can claim I haven't been doing extracurricular activities after work hours. Speaking of work hours, what case are you working on?"

"Remember that case we did a couple of years ago on the Davison twins? Well, it's finally gone to trial and Dr. Fitzgerald wants us to shore up our testimony to include a rebuttal argument that all identical twins have the same DNA."

I nod. "It makes sense. Most people don't know about phenotypes. So, I'll put together something to explain how identical twins can be different —" I freeze as a chill goes up my spine. I have a feeling of dread in my stomach as I look around the small coffee shop.

Jamie notices my inattention to our conversation. "Dakota, are you okay? You seem distracted."

"I can't get over the feeling I'm being watched. It's creeping me out."

Jamie studies everyone in the coffee shop. "I don't see anything. Do you want to go back to your suite?"

I nod. "My gut tells me something is very, very wrong."

"What do you think? Should I leave this slide in my testimony or do you think it's confusing?"

Jamie scoots closer and holds his hand up to shield the computer screen from the sunlight streaming in through the beautiful historic windows of my Sweetwater suite.

"Looks good to me. But make sure you change the names. This slide lists the case name as Schofield. You'll have to give yourself some additional time to walk the jurors through this one. The way I see it, this is the crux of the case. Take your time and go through every element."

"Good point, let me fix that now before I forget." As I start to make corrections, the door to the suite opens.

I glance up to see a thunderous expression on Nick's face. "Am I interrupting something here?" he snaps.

Jamie and I look at each other in disbelief. "Umm … no, we're just working on a case," Jamie stammers.

"Oh, is that what they're calling it these days?" He glares at me. "You know, I thought you were the opposite of Cheryl. I guess I was wrong."

"I don't know what you're reading into this situation but it's dead wrong." I have to pause for a moment to catch my breath and wipe away tears.

Jamie stands up and goes toe to toe with Nick. "I don't

know who you are or who you think Dakota is, but your way off base here. I am not, nor have I ever been dating, Dr. Crenshaw. Let me tell you, it's not for lack of trying. She's just not interested in me. She made that abundantly clear when we first started working together and her mind hasn't been changed in four years. So, if she's not interested in being with me when she didn't have a boyfriend, she sure as heck isn't interested now. In fact, most of our conversations involve a few words about how awesome she thinks you are. If you think I'm competing with you, you can stand down. You've already won the competition."

Nick takes a step back and glances over at me. "Is this guy right?"

I nod. "Dr. Jamie Douglas is going to make a great partner for somebody — but that person is not me."

"You didn't tell me you were going to have company," Nick presses.

"I know this looks bad. But nothing nefarious was going on. Dakota and I originally met at a little sandwich place to work on our trial presentation, but she got creeped out by some guy who was watching her. She said she would feel more comfortable working from the Sweetwater."

Nick's demeanor suddenly changes. He is now completely alert in a different way. "Who was following you? Have you seen him before?"

When he asks that question, the blood drains out of my face. "Remember the other day when I had such a bad headache? I went to a nearby drugstore to get some pain medication. I think that same guy was lurking around."

"Wow! I hope you are wrong, Dakota. That's down right weird. Why would a guy who looks to be about sixty-five be following you around?" Jamie asks.

"I know this is going to sound strange given my misconceptions and jealous reaction to your friend here, but please don't go anywhere without me, Pauline, Cody or Tristan. It's really important."

"Nick, what aren't you telling me? Do you know who this guy is?"

"I don't — at least not yet. Before I say anything more, I need to confirm some suspicions and have Tristan check them out. Please be careful." Nick looks over at Jamie. "I know I am the new guy in Dakota's life, but I intend to stay in it for a long time."

Jamie nods. "Message received loud and clear. Keep Dakota safe."

I look around at my surroundings and have to pinch myself. Cody and Dylan are coming up with a game plan as we fly to Tennessee on Tristan's plane. He is up talking to the pilot. Finally, I look at Pauline and ask, "Do you ever feel like you've been dropped in the middle of a crime show and you're the only one without a script?"

"Sometimes, every day feels like that for me. It doesn't happen so much anymore, but when I first started, I was one of the youngest recruits to join the force. Many folks thought I had a leg up because my dad was a respected detective. At first, I would skip steps without meaning to. I figured I already knew what to do. Sometimes, that worked in my favor, other times it got me temporarily suspended."

"Oh wow! I don't want to do anything to jeopardize this operation. But I don't really know what to do. I'm just the scientist who works in a think tank. I'm afraid I'm going to mess everything up."

Frank smiles and pats me on the knee. "For a newcomer, you're doing just fine. So, what do you want to know?"

"I'm just not sure how you all want me to contribute. The DNA matches have already been established and presumably we've found out the identity of Baby Jane Doe. I don't understand how I can help the case at this point."

Toby glances over at me. "I get where you're coming from, but sometimes people need to be convinced that the science is telling us the truth. That's where you come in. Dylan, Cody, and Pauline have the law enforcement contingent covered. As a former profiler, Frank is really good at breaking through people's BS. He'll know if they are lying. Phoenix isn't here, but he and I have been working on connecting all the clues and coming up with a theory of the case."

Nick leans forward. "Okay, so let me ask the obvious question. Why am I here?"

Frank laughs out loud. "Like I said, you are the ideal agitator. Your friends and family are likely coming into these interviews with their story already set. I'm hoping your presence on our team will shake 'em up a little and encourage them to tell the truth."

Cody twirls his pen as he listens to the conversation. "I gotta warn you, as much as you think you know where this interrogation is going to go, it will probably veer off course into places you'd rather not be. These are people who you loved at one point in your life even if it doesn't feel like you still are connected with them. That's going to make your emotions volatile. To the best of your ability, you need to contain those emotions and treat these suspects as if they are total strangers."

Cody looks directly at me as he adds, "You are the voice of logic and scientific focus here. As much as you love Nick, you can't be giving him supportive looks and reassuring touches. The two of you need to act as if you are essentially strangers."

Dylan nods. "I speak from the voice of experience. Even though I had several years of law enforcement experience under my belt before I became involved with Lauren's family when we were trying to solve her sister's disappearance, it was difficult to stay objective and focus on just the outcome. If it becomes too intense for you, you need to let us know so we can remove you from the situation before it blows up in our face."

Nick nods thoughtfully. "I will try my best to keep a lid on it. I'm aware that giving my brother a black eye wasn't particularly helpful in moving the investigation forward. I'll try to keep my hands to myself. The other part of your advice is a little tougher to follow. If I see Dakota struggling, I'm going to want to help her — no two ways about it."

"We can help each other out as teammates, but it has to look as if that's all we are — all of us," Dylan replies.

Pauline winks at Dylan. "Does that mean I can't make out with my husband in the middle of the case?"

Cody chokes back his laughter. "Rookie, I've seen you on far too many undercover operations to question your methods. If you think it will help, go for it."

Toby shoots his wife a stricken look. "I love you honey, but don't do that to me. I need to focus on collecting data to solve Harmony Hope's murder."

Pauline sticks her tongue out at her husband. "I was

kidding! The middle of an interrogation is not the time to think about romance."

Dylan blushes. "I don't know. I thought a lot about Lauren at some pretty inopportune times."

Cody plugs his ears. "TMI partner, TMI!"

"Okay, you say that. But I remember when you were working with your wife to solve the kidnappings, you were not always focused entirely on the case."

Cody puts his hands in front of him in a gesture of innocence. "You're not wrong. So, guys try to do as we say and not as we do. It'll make this case go much faster and my buddy here wants to marry his fiancée sooner rather than later. Lauren has been waiting a long time to have her day."

Frank studies me intently. "You feeling better about things?"

I blow out a deep breath as I do a little self-reflection.

"Yeah, I think I am. I've got parameters to work with now. Thank you so much."

"You're welcome Dr. Crenshaw. We're glad you're on our team. Let's get ready to catch a child murderer. Whoever it is, they need to be off the street."

Nick reaches across the armrest and squeezes my hand. "Amen to that. I just hope the outcome doesn't destroy my mother."

"Just remember, whatever the outcome is, you are not responsible for the actions of the people you love."

Nick leans over and kisses me on the cheek. "I know that, but thanks for the reminder."

Next time I see Tristan, I'm going to hug him for letting us use his plane. I've never slept well while flying, but Tristan's plane is positively decadent. I even got to nap in a real bed. A voice interrupts my reminiscing. "Howdy, y'all must be from the Cold Case Squadron. I am Chief Greenborough."

Dylan shakes the local sheriff's hand before we walk down the hall to a large conference room. "Chief Greenborough, we appreciate the use of your facilities. Your cooperation makes the work of the Cold Case Squadron go much smoother. "

The chief nods solemnly. "Anything we can do to help bring closure to Baby Jane Doe. That child has touched our whole community. We need to find who killed her."

"That's what we're aiming to do here," Dylan replies.

The chief flips on the light in the conference room. "I wish you all the best of luck. I'll get out of here. You holler if you need something. If you need to record your session, the switch with the yellow button turns on the video camera system. When you are ready for the persons of interest, just send me a text message and I'll have our officers escort them all in. It's my understanding you want them all at once, correct?"

"That's the plan," Pauline answers with a genuine smile.

"Ambitious, but I like it," the chief answers.

"Sometimes you gotta make big plays to get big results."

The chief nods tightly at our group. "Understood. Just let me know when you want them."

Dylan nods. "Will do."

As we gather around the table, Frank points out a chair. "Dr. Crenshaw I'm going to put you here and Nick will be directly across the table from you. From you, Dr. Crenshaw, I want science and more science to refute any false assertions."

Nick chuckles. "You weren't kidding about keeping us apart, were you?"

Frank shakes his head. "Nope. This may appear chaotic, but there is a method to our madness." He looks at Pauline. "When was the last time you played the good cop, Rookie?"

Pauline blows her hair out of her face. "It's been a while. But I can do that if you want me to."

"I want someone Cheryl can bond with. Maybe she'll be persuaded to tell the truth if she thinks you're on her side."

Pauline sits down in the chair beside me. "I understand. But just for the record, if she killed this baby, she and I have nothing in common — pretend or otherwise."

"That goes without saying. Cody, if this degenerates into a fight between exes, you're responsible for pointing the conversation back to the science and what happened to Harmony Hope."

Dylan takes a seat next to Nick. "I guess that makes me the pressure guy?"

Frank nods. "You got it. Toby will collect data and I'll observe all the interactions. I hope to be able to determine who is telling the truth and who is lying to cover their butts.

Dylan looks around the table. "Everybody clear on the

plan?"

We all nod. My stomach lurches uncomfortably. This one interview could make or break this case.

Dylan pulls out his cell phone and starts to type. "Very well, let's get this show on the road."

Milo is the first to be brought into the conference room. He looks a little startled to see Nick there. "I guess family loyalty doesn't mean much, huh?" he comments to his brother.

Nick studiously ignores him. I can see his jaw clench so I know this is taking a toll.

Next Cheryl comes in the room. I notice today she is wearing yoga pants and an oversized T-shirt and her makeup isn't done impeccably like it was the last time we encountered her.

"What's he doing here?" she hisses as soon as she sees Milo. "He didn't want anything to do with Harmony Hope. Maybe he's the reason she's dead!"

Milo takes the bait. "How in the world could I be responsible for killing a child I didn't know existed until after she was already dead?"

"You knew she existed! I sent you a letter a week before I went into labor with her. You didn't even bother to respond to me. You created her, but you didn't give a rats butt what happened to her. I could've died in labor and you wouldn't have blinked an eye."

"How was I supposed to know you were telling the truth? I thought you were just trying to split me up with

Shalonda. You told me you would do anything to make sure we were together. I just thought this was another one of your lies."

"Why would I lie to you about a child? I know that you wanted to be a dad. You talked about how hard it was for you and her to conceive a baby. I thought a baby was what you wanted?"

"I did want a baby! I wanted to have a child with my wife."

"If you wanted your wife so much, why did you mess around with me?"

"You know the answer to that. Shalonda was incredibly depressed after the last round of IVF failed. I was feeling lonely and neglected. You took advantage of our friendship and turned it into something it should have never been."

I shoot a glance across the table at Nick after Milo made that blunt assessment of his relationship with Cheryl. He looks ready to punch his brother again.

Dylan looks at both Cheryl and Milo. "As fascinating as this little soap opera is, it's not getting us any closer to answers about what happened to your daughter. Dr. Crenshaw, why don't you update Mrs. Long and Mr. Weston on the status of the case?"

I clear my throat and hand Milo and Cheryl the results of the DNA tests. "I understand this is probably information you both know. But for the integrity of the case, I need to inform you that you are the parents of Baby Jane Doe also known as Harmony Hope. We found Harmony Hope at the bottom of a well in Owl Creek, Tennessee. Based on what you've already told members of this task force, we believe Harmony Hope was killed shortly after she disappeared. Unfortunately, her remains were too degraded to determine the cause of death. We do know the death was a homicide."

"Are you sure she didn't just wander off and fall into the well?"

I flinch when he asks that question. "Yes, we are certain someone killed your daughter. There was duct tape around her wrists, ankles and mouth."

Cheryl abruptly stands up and throws up in the garbage can in the corner of the room. Pauline takes some cold water from the small fridge and hands it to her. "Are you all right?" she asks gently.

"No! I'm not all right," Cheryl says as she sits back down in her chair. She takes a swig of water and wipes away tears. "My daughter is gone. I thought she was safe with Milo! I got a note and everything from him saying she was safe. Instead, he killed her!"

"I did not kill our daughter. I didn't even know she was real. I thought she was a figment of your imagination because you were trying to convince me to stay with you. I didn't even know I could have kids! Shalonda and I tried for years without success. You can't accuse me of killing a child I had no idea was real."

Pauline tries to direct the conversation. "Cheryl, can you tell us why you believe Milo killed Harmony?"

"It had to be him. I wrote him a letter begging for help. George was beating me up every single day. I was afraid he was doing things to Harmony too. So, I decided to leave. But I knew I couldn't go on the run with a toddler. I didn't have the money to keep her safe. So, I wrote to Milo asking for his help. He wrote me back and said she'd be taken care of."

Milo shakes his head. "I didn't get a letter like that! I'm not a monster. If I had gotten that kind of letter, I would've helped. After all, she was our daughter."

I catch a pained expression as it crosses Nick's face.

"Cheryl, where did you deliver that letter?" Nick presses.

It's as if Cheryl finally discovers Nick's presence in the room. She looks up at him in shock. "Oh my gosh! I am so sorry. It was stupid of me to get involved with your brother. You've got to believe me, I've grown up so much. I know there's way more to a successful relationship than whether your partner is home for every birthday, anniversary and holiday. I'm sorry I blew such a good thing with you."

Nick looks uncomfortable with the apology. "Cheryl, I used to think what I had with you was sacred and beautiful. Obviously it wasn't and you moved on to greener pastures. This here," he says as he gestures around the room, "it isn't about us or even who we could have been together, this is about finding who murdered your daughter. So, where did you mail your letter?"

Cheryl rolls her shoulder. "I didn't actually mail the letter. I delivered it in person. I went to my grandma's house to get some money. She gave me a little bit of cash to help me escape from George. Your brother lived close by and I just dropped the letter in his mailbox."

Dylan looks sharply at Milo. "Who had access to that mailbox?"

Milo drops his head. "Just me and my wife."

Dylan leans forward and scoots his chair up to where his knees are almost touching Milo's. "Okay, this is what I think happened. You got the letter and panicked. You decided you would get rid of your daughter before your wife found out about your indiscretions. That's how it went down, wasn't it?"

Milo shoots to his feet. "No! That's not what happened. Until you guys confronted me with the DNA, I had no idea that my daughter was a real human being. I would've never done anything to harm her. No marriage is worth saving if it costs the life of a child."

"If you didn't do it, who do you think did?" Cody asks.

I push my notebook aside and toss my pen on the table. "The only logical suspect is Cheryl's ex. She said he was violent and hurting her. So, it makes sense that he would hurt my neice to keep Cheryl from leaving."

Cheryl shakes her head. "He was at work right up until the point the police officers brought him in on domestic abuse charges. The dumb jerk got killed in a knife fight in jail. I can't say I miss him but I know he didn't do anything to Harmony Hope. He couldn't have."

Pauline picks up an ink pen and a pad of paper. "Where was Harmony Hope while you were preparing to leave George?"

"I left her at my grandma's house."

Nick scrubs his hand down his face, and whispers, "Please tell me you don't mean Helen." Louder, he says, "Cheryl, is this the same grandma who is friends with my mom? The one with dementia?"

Cheryl wipes away tears and nods. "It's not like I had lots of places to put her. In order to get away from George, I had to borrow someone's car. One of my friends from high school let me have her beater car. I was planning to go all the way to California where no one could find us. But when I got back from getting new tires on the car,

Harmony Hope was gone from her playpen at my grandma's house. MawMaw couldn't remember what happened to her."

Nick groans and rubs his temple, but Cheryl continues.

"When I got the letter saying she was safe, I just assumed you had gotten my letter and came over to get her. George sent me a text message from his job. He threatened to kill me because we were behind on the utility bill. So, I took that as a sign from God and just got the heck out of there. I got as far as New Mexico before the car broke down. I stayed there until I heard from the district attorney that George had been killed in jail. Then I came back home."

Milo shakes his head. "I don't know what letter you're talking about, but I didn't write to you at all."

Pauline looks shaken by Cheryl's story. "So, your child just disappeared and you didn't think to look for her or to check in with her father to see if she was doing okay?"

"I know it sounds stupid now, but I was in self preservation mode. I had the letter, so I let myself believe Milo and Shalonda were taking good care of my daughter and I didn't want to interrupt that. So, I didn't look for her I thought she was living happily ever after. After a while, I decided I needed to move on too. I felt like a failure as a mother, so I never even told Bubba that Harmony existed. As far as he knows, my ex-husband died of a heart attack."

Nick's expression hardens. "Don't you ever get tired of the lies? Or, do you like having a bunch of men at your beck and call?"

Cheryl throws up her hands. "What was I supposed to tell him? I had a daughter because I was sleeping with my boyfriend's brother in order to make him jealous? On top of that, I don't even know where my daughter is? That would make me sound insane."

"It is insane!" bellows Milo. "Why would I take a child I knew nothing about? It doesn't make any sense. You had to have done something to her."

"I didn't. Okay, I wasn't the best mom because I let George into our life and he was dangerous. I was trying to keep my daughter safe. That's why I ran away. I contacted you because I knew you would do the right thing. You always do the right thing — that's why you went back to Shalonda. I thought you were keeping her safe."

Dylan steeples his fingers in front of his chin. "If we believe the stories as you two tell them, we are overlooking a suspect. If neither of you killed your daughter and George was unable to do so, that leaves one person with access to the mailbox."

Nick's jaw drops. "Holy crap! You think Shalonda did it?"

Frank nods. "She fits the profile. You said she was depressed because of failed fertility treatments. I believe Cheryl disclosed she thought that Shalonda knew about the relationship. If Shalonda thought Milo would stay with Cheryl because of the baby, she might have decided to remove her from the equation."

"That can't be right. Shalonda loves children. She would go to the hospital and hold premature babies and she volunteered at our local church nursery every week. There's no way Shalonda could have done something like this. She was so desperate to have a child, she wouldn't be capable of killing one," Milo insists.

"You would be surprised at what people are capable of when they're backed into a corner," Frank replies.

Milo runs his hand through his hair. "As much as I hate to admit it, that would explain a lot. Around that time, Shalonda's dependence on prescription medication skyrocketed. A lot of the things she was saying didn't make any sense. Finally, her doctor admitted her to the psychiatric unit to treat her depression."

"What happened next?" Cody asks.

Milo sighs. "I thought this was bizarre at the time. But Shalonda's therapist decided I was a toxic influence in her life and convinced Shalonda to divorce me. I knew things weren't working out between us, although, I never really knew why. Shalonda was fixated on making sure I was able to pass along my genes even though I told her that adoption would be just fine. It was so hard to see her fight through every cycle of IVF and have it fail."

"That's tough," Pauline admits.

"Yeah, I just figured that there was so much pain between us that maybe our marriage was the casualty. I never imagined that the real casualty would be my wife's sanity." He turns to Cheryl. "If Shalonda did something to our daughter, I'm so, so sorry. What you and I did together was wrong. But Harmony didn't deserve to die for our mistakes."

Cheryl takes a tissue from the middle of the conference table and dabs at her eyes. "I've made so many mistakes I don't even know where to go from here. You have to know I didn't kill our daughter and I don't know for sure who did. But I'm afraid Shalonda makes a really good suspect."

Frank makes a big showing of closing his notebook. "I think we have a direction to go from here. Thank you all for being so honest and forthright. It is our goal to get justice for your daughter. We intend to continue that mission.”

“So you’re going to question Shalonda next?” I clarify.

“Good luck with that,” Milo comments. “My divorce attorneys have been trying to locate her without any luck.”

Toby is rapidly typing on his computer. “I don’t have an exact address yet, but it looks like Mrs. Weston is located in a small town on the Connecticut border.”

Dylan nods. “Well, I guess we have our marching orders. Thank you for your time everyone.”

Cheryl tearfully addresses the group, “I’m sorry I made such a mess of things. I never meant to hurt Milo or Nick. Nick had been in my corner for as long as I can remember. I’m sorry I disrespected that. Maybe I deserve what happened to Harmony Hope.”

Nick shakes his head. “Cheryl, you made a massive miscalculation. Who knows, maybe we would’ve made it … and maybe we were never meant to be. But regardless, no one deserves to have their child murdered.”

The relief on her face is evident. “I’m so sorry I drove you away. You were always one of the good guys.”

I fight the urge to say something like your loss is my gain.

She turns to Milo. “I am the saddest for you. You would’ve made a terrific father. I should have handled a million things differently than I did. I’m sorry I robbed you of that opportunity.”

Milo swallows hard. “Unfortunately, there isn’t an apology on the planet that will bring our daughter back. I wish things would’ve been handled differently too. Because now I have to face the prospect that the woman I have loved for more than a decade murdered my child. I don't even know how to wrap my brain around that."

Nick stands up and walks over to give Milo a hug. "I'm sorry big brother. Whatever happens, just know I love you and have your back."

# CHAPTER TWENTY

# NICK

As soon as we enter the hotel suite, Dakota walks over and places her arms around me and squeezes tightly. "I'm so sorry. I know that's not how you wanted it to go."

I lean down and kiss her forehead. She takes my hand and leads me to the love seat. She gracefully tucks her feet under her as she urges me to sit beside her.

"How are you doing?" she asks gently.

I shrug. "Honestly, I don't know. I can't get one thought out of my brain. I can't believe I didn't know Cheryl better than that. I've been in love with her since I was about thirteen. I thought I knew who she was — inside and out. The Cheryl we saw today at the interrogation doesn't resemble the Cheryl I fell in love with. She would've never just given up a child and thrown up her hands and said, 'Oh well, I hope she ended up in a good home.' Who does that? I wouldn't even do that to a puppy, let alone a toddler who can't speak for herself."

Dakota strokes my shoulder. "I don't understand what she did either. I can't imagine simply throwing away a child. Then again, I've never been in a physically abusive relationship."

Something in Dakota's tone makes the hair on the back of my neck stand up. "But … you've been in other abusive relationships?"

A look of pain crosses Dakota's face. "Yeah. After I went through everything with my father, I swore up and down I would never accept anyone into my life who abuses me. Yet, I did just that in college."

I place my arm around her shoulder and snuggle her against my chest. "I'm sorry you went through that."

"I'm lucky it wasn't worse. I was just so naïve. When Thomas Madden started paying attention to me during my freshman year in college, I was beyond flattered. Where I grew up, all the kids in my class were familiar with the fire and what it did to my body. When I got to college, with some creative clothing choices, no one had to know my tragic back story."

"I know what you mean. When my dad died, everyone seemed to know and instantly judge me for his actions."

Dakota nods. "Exactly. Everyone has their own theory about why things happen. So, anyway, when Thomas started flirting with me, I fell hard. At first, it was wonderful. We were both math geeks and we did all of our homework together. Soon, Thomas stopped doing his and expected me to complete it for him. Initially, I was flattered that he trusted me to do something so important. I didn't understand what was going on until the teacher's assistant called me out on what I was doing and explained to me how Thomas was exploiting me."

I nod against the top of her head. "Yeah, that was a really scummy thing to do."

"I'm lucky it didn't get me kicked out of college. At

first, I didn't want to believe what she was saying to me. Then, I started paying attention to what Thomas was actually asking me to do and how he reacted if I refused. It started to scare me, so eventually I broke it off."

"Good for you!" I hug her tightly.

"That's what I'm saying. Eventually I got there, but it took me an embarrassingly long time to get out of that situation. I can only imagine it would be exponentially worse if someone was physically abusing me and I needed to protect my child."

"I think that's the thing that bugs me the most. She didn't protect her daughter. It seems like she didn't even try."

"I know, that bothers me too. I'd like to think if I had a child, I would move heaven and earth to protect her. For a long time, I was mad at my mother for staying with Sheldon. I swore I would never find myself in the same situation, but eventually I did."

My spine stiffens and I glare at Dakota. "Are you defending her?"

"No! I think what she did is wrong. I'm just saying we haven't walked in her shoes. The situation might look different through her eyes."

"Make no mistake, I'm mad at Milo too. He could have avoided this whole situation if he'd just kept his pants zipped."

"I get that too. But I feel sorry for your brother. He didn't have any reason to believe Cheryl when she told him she was pregnant. For all he knew, he couldn't even have children. I'm not sure I would have acted any differently in his shoes."

I nod slowly as I ponder her words. "Yeah, Cheryl has

a way of wrapping you around her pinky finger and leading you where she wants to go. I should know, I spent years blindly following her. Maybe I shouldn't be so hard on Milo. Cheryl can be mighty persuasive."

"Hopefully, Shalonda will be able to provide the missing pieces. I understand Toby is still trying to track her down."

I groan. "I spent lots of time away from Milo and Shalonda. I didn't know her very well, but I know my mama was really attached to her. My mom always regretted that she didn't have any girls. So when Milo and I got old enough to date, she always treated our girlfriends like they were her kids too. This is going to break her heart."

Dakota brushes her fingers down my cheek. "That's terrible. There is far too much pain to go around."

"Honestly, it's a good thing we have a few days for all this to sink in and something happy to look forward to in the meantime. My soul feels like it has a thousand cracks in it. I need some time to heal before taking on Shalonda."

Just as I brush a kiss across Dakota's lips, the door swings open. Ketki shakes her head in disgust. "Not you guys too! It's like kissing is a disease around here."

I step in front of Dakota. "I'm sorry Ketki. I will try not to embarrass you anymore. Can you forgive me?" I bow deeply and present Ketki with a huge bouquet of yellow roses interspersed with colorful bird feathers. "Congratulations Ketki, I know you worked really hard for this."

Ketki starts jumping up and down with glee. "Hey

Dad! I finally got flowers from a boy. He even remembered I love feathers."

Dakota comes out from behind me and hands Ketki a brightly wrapped present. "Thanks for inviting us."

Ketki's brows furrow when she sees Dakota. "I'm sorry I shouldn't have said that about the flowers. That's pretty weird since he's your boyfriend."

Dakota grins. "That's okay. I don't mind if Nick gets flowers for his friends. I think it's sweet. Besides, he gave me a beautiful bouquet this morning. He gave me red and pink ones."

"My Grandma Nancy says red roses means somebody loves you and yellow roses means they just want to be friends. She was telling me there's a whole language when it comes to flowers. It's sorta like math equations."

"I guess it could be like that," Dakota concedes. "Whatever they mean, I love getting flowers."

Ketki pulls Dakota into the large meeting room at Identity Bank. "You're not gonna believe what Tristan did for my graduation. He offered me a ride to anywhere in the whole world on his airplane, but I don't really like planes so he created something here for me that I absolutely love." Ketki gestures around the humongous room.

Dakota high-fives her. "Sweet! I've never seen an arcade as decked out as this. I mean, some of these games I recognize from when I was growing up. But others are so new I've never played them."

"That's because Tristan and my stepdad have been working on some of these games for years. Tristan is letting me debut his new role playing game here. Isn't that cool? You can even play it with your eyes closed or with only one hand. John has been working really hard to make it accessible to everyone."

"That's great! Everyone should be able to play."

Ketki reaches toward me and pulls me into the corner. "Look! He put one of your favorite kind of games in here too. You can fly anything you want to in virtual reality. This game is so realistic it makes me dizzy when I play it. Isn't that amazing?"

I smile widely because Ketki's enthusiasm and endless questions are infectious. You can't help but be happy around her.

Suddenly she frowns. "It's not all good news though. My friend Jason was supposed to come, but his grandma got sick and he had to go visit her in Colorado. So, he can't come. I mean, I want to understand why he changed his mind, but it seems like maybe he was just looking for a reason not to come to my party. That part makes me sad."

I place my arm around her shoulders being careful to respect her personal space. "You know, sometimes people with good excuses are actually telling the truth. Maybe he really did have to visit a sick grandmother."

Ketki shrugs. "Maybe, but I'm not going to bank on it. I've had lots of friends tell me they were going to hang out with me and then change their mind."

"I'm sorry. That must be disappointing. But don't worry, you have lots of friends here."

Ketki turns to me. "Is it weird having a postgraduation party where you work?" Ketki asks. "My parents are so silly. Who gets two parties for their graduation?"

I smile. "Definitely made my commute easier because I knew exactly where to park. No, seriously I think you have the most epic parties I've ever been to. Not very many people get to set up their own private arcade and play games all night."

Ketki gives me a quizzical look. "You haven't hung out with me much have you? This is pretty much all my friends and I do."

When we enter the room, Ketki's dad, Mark hits the side of his glass with a spoon. Of course, it doesn't make much noise because it's plastic. So, Ketki's Aunt Savannah whistles sharply to get everyone's attention. "I think it's time for the guest of honor to start us out with a speech."

Ketki blanches. "Are you sure people want to hear what I have to say? I'm not very good at speaking in front of people."

Mark reaches his hand out toward his daughter. "You can do this. Just pretend it's like ringing the bell of prosperity at Ink'd Deep."

"Yeah, that would've been cool. But Jade said Ink'd Deep isn't big enough to have this kind of party."

"No problem, girlfriend," Jade responds as she tucks a bright turquoise shock of hair behind her ear. "Anytime this group of people get together, it's a built-in party. Besides, you and I have an appointment at Ink'd Deep later."

Declan starts pounding on a desk to create a drumroll.

Mark lifts Ketki up and sets her on a table as if it is a stage. She rolls her eyes at him. "Dad! I'm an adult now. You don't have to do that."

"You don't have to remind me, I'm having enough difficulties as it is coping with the fact that my beautiful, smart, funny daughter has grown up into such a lovely lady. I know you hear this all the time, but you are the spitting image of your mother when Tayanita was your age."

Ketki's mother looks embarrassed. "Our daughter might look like me, but she is just like you and Shelby. I couldn't have chosen a better mother for my daughter."

"Hey, I thought this was supposed to be my speech. You're taking my material!" Ketki insists as she places her hand on her hip.

Ketki pretends to tap on a microphone. "Okay, I just want to say thank you to everyone who came to my party tonight. Everyone here has done something to help me along the way." She points to Jessica and Mitch. "You helped me understand that even though I felt like my mom didn't love me, I might not understand both sides of the story. You also made it okay for me to love my cats more than I like people. I'm getting a little better at that but I have to say some days I'd rather just be around my animals."

Mitch, Jessica's husband, who runs Hope's Haven rescue and training facility, smiles. "It's not just you. Stuart and I feel the same way sometimes."

The blond veterinarian with spiky hair grins. "You mean I'm not supposed to prefer animals over people? I guess I didn't get the memo."

Ketki plows ahead. "When I was little, I was pretty lonely because it was just my dad and me. Then Shelby came into our lives. She's the first person I ever knew who loves math as much as me. Not only that, she gets me. She understands that I like stones and feathers and puzzles. She never tries to change me or make me feel bad for being different. I'm so glad my dad fell in love with her because I did too."

Shelby wipes away tears. "Why would I want to change you? You're perfect just the way you are."

"I'm glad my dad fell in love with Shelby. Not just because I wanted her to be my mom but because she helped bring my birth mom back into my life. I am so lucky I have four parents who love and support me."

Ketki looks over at John and Tuffy. "John, I'll never forget when my mom first introduced me to you. I was so confused. I didn't understand how we were going to go for a hike when you couldn't see where we were going. It didn't make any sense to me. But you showed me how to celebrate the things in life I didn't even know I was looking for. You gave me the courage to go down unfamiliar paths. I am so glad you're my stepdad."

John clears his throat and swallows a couple of times before he begins speaking. "After my accident, nothing in my world was familiar. For a while, I thought my life as I knew it was over. But then I found your mom and you. Both of you quietly make it easier for me to live with my blindness. Look at you, Lady Gogo is coming right along and you encouraged Tristan to start a new branch of his business. Without you and your creative vision, I wouldn't have a job I love at Identity Bank. Thank you for accepting me into your life. Being your stepdad is a huge honor."

Ketki looks at the wall across from where she's speaking. I've been around her long enough to know she is fighting to regain her composure. "Thank you for accepting me and never pretending to let me win at chess. That little thing spoke volumes about how much you respect who I am as a person. I know many of you have questions about what I plan to do next. I've thought long and hard about this."

Shelby looks startled. "Have you accepted an offer from one of the colleges? You know, your dad and I need to make some plans."

"I know." Ketki turns toward her mom. "I know you were worried that I might go to Stanford or Berkeley. I mean, their scholarship offers were amazing. But I'm not sure I'm ready for that."

Mark walks closer to the table where she's standing. "It's okay sweetheart, there are no wrong answers. You have to do what's right for you."

Ketki blows out a deep breath. "Oh boy, I'm so glad you said that. Because I don't know what you'll say about what I've decided. But I think it's the best for me. I talked to Tristan. He's going to offer me a half-time job at Identity Bank."

John glowers. "Did I hear you right? Did you say part time?"

"I did. I've been part of his gaming division for quite some time. I have pretty much been helping him program for years. So, he's going to put me in charge of managing product testing teams like the one I started out on."

Shelby looks at her stepdaughter with fear and trepidation on her face. "That's only half time. What are you going to do the rest of the time?"

Ketki smiles, "That's the best part. I was talking to Dakota and Nick about how worried I was that I might choose the wrong path. So, Tristan says I can work at Identity Bank and go to Santa Fe College part-time. I can take as many different classes as I need to decide where I feel the most comfortable. If it's somewhere else, other than the gaming industry, Tristan says he'll give me a generous severance package when I'm ready to fly the coop."

Jade smiles. "I support that approach. If things would have gone differently, I might have chosen to be a teacher.

What do you think you want to explore?"

Ketki looks at Dakota. "I kind of like what Dakota does. She is smart like me and loves math puzzles, but she gets to help law enforcement from behind-the-scenes. As much fun as I had helping Savannah and Cody catch those catfishing pedophiles, that was too much pressure for me. I don't think I'd like to do that every day. But I liked working for the good guys. So, I'm going to explore ways to do that."

Mark looks at his daughter wistfully. "I was kind of hoping you would follow in my footsteps and become a lawyer. You've been phenomenal at asking questions ever since you were old enough to talk. You could argue some veteran attorneys under the table."

Ketki grins. "Don't worry, Dad, I haven't ruled that out. I might also become a teacher like Shelby. If it wasn't for her, the bullies could have won. But if she can beat skin cancer, I can deal with my autism and be tough."

Mark reaches up and pulls his daughter off the desk. He spins her around in a tight hug. "Whatever happens, you have to know I'm incredibly proud of the woman you've become. It's okay with us if you stay home and don't go away to school. We want you to be happy."

Ketki, in a rare display of affection brushes a kiss across Mark's cheek. "Stop stressing. That's what this whole experiment is about. I'm trying to find what makes me truly happy. Like Dakota says, even if I choose wrong, I can always pick a different path later."

Tayanita meets Dakota's gaze. "That sounds like very sage advice. I'm glad you have such amazing friends."

Dakota reaches out and grabs my hand. She smiles as she watches Ketki.

"Umm, anyway I didn't really have a whole speech planned or anything I just wanted to let you all know what I was thinking. Thank you so much for being my friends and showing up tonight. I don't have anything more to say. So, I guess we should eat the cake my Grandma Nancy made and start playing these games. You know, they won't play themselves. Well, technically some of them do but that's a whole other issue. Let's go have ourselves a party."

I squeeze Dakota's hand and pull her close for a quick kiss. She blushes as she asks, "What was that for?"

Before I kiss her again, I murmur, "Ketki said this is a party to celebrate the people who have made a difference in her life. I want you to know how much better you've made my life."

As we break apart, she responds, "I love being here with you, but I feel bad. My presence has been like a wrecking ball for your family."

I pull her close and kiss the top of her head. "Don't feel bad. My ex and my brother's actions have nothing to do with us. We are all about finding hope in the middle of chaos. What happens to them doesn't change our love story."

I feel someone tap me on my shoulder. Ketki is studying us carefully. "Actually, if it's bad, it could ruin everything," she announces starkly. "When things get hard, remember what you said tonight. You need to deal with your past before you can move forward. It's really important."

I'm tempted to make a joke about her strange instructions, but Ketki looks so solemn, I just nod. "I'll try."

She breathes a sigh of relief and then drags me toward

the back corner. "It's not often someone else is better at video games than me. This is the first time I have seen this kind of simulator. Will you show me how to make it work?"

Years of practice in simulators and in real life flash before my eyes including the crash which almost took my ability to walk.

Dakota senses my discomfort. "You never know who you'll be inspiring. Ketki may be a next generation soldier who makes it possible for America to win wars without sacrificing pilots on the ground. Go show your stuff. I'm sure you're itching to touch the controls again."

I blow out a deep breath. "You always know the perfect thing to say. There would be no greater honor to my service and the service of my grandfather than to train a better more efficient Army."

Ketki has a bewildered expression on her face. "Geez, Nick … I just asked you to teach me to play a video game. I'm not planning to enlist or anything."

I grin. "Yeah, but you never know. You know the best and the brightest and all that. Let me go show you what it's like to fly as free as a bird."

# Chapter Twenty-One

# Dakota

I look around the bright contemporary tattoo studio. Someday I might be brave enough to do what Ketki is doing today. I would like to cover up some of my more obvious scars and turn them into badges of survival. However, to do that I need to overcome my fear of needles. That may not happen anytime soon.

I look over at Ketki who it is chilling out to some seventies music through her headphones. When she sees me looking at her, she takes them off. "What?"

"Well, honestly I'm glad you're my friend, but I wonder why I'm here instead of Shelby or Tayanita."

"My mom was supposed to come, but she got called into work in the ER. The design of the tattoo is a surprise to Shelby and my dad. I mean, they figure feathers will be involved but they don't know the rest of the design. Anyway, I thought you would be the best person to keep a secret."

"I am honored you chose me to come with you. Maybe I will get brave enough to get my own tattoo someday."

"If you hang around this group long enough, you

won't have much choice. Almost everybody has some kind of tattoo. My dad has a huge dream catcher on his back. Ever since he got it, I wanted Jade to give me a matching tattoo." Ketki pulls a sketch up on her iPad. "Isn't this cool? It has feathers like my dad's dream catcher. These stones represent my family. Everyone is unique and different. Some are Cherokee and other people are *unega*,-- umm … I mean white like you. But all the people in my life help make me who I am. The wispy clouds around the tattoo represent all the things I think about that don't bother other people."

"What do you mean?"

"You might have noticed that I don't really like crowds and noise. Processing all of it makes me dizzy and nauseous. So, I close my eyes and cover my ears. I have to make order of things. So, I like to line up puzzle pieces, feathers, stones or nail polish colors. It doesn't matter. As long as I can rearrange things so it makes sense to me, I feel calmer. That's why Jade is doing those clouds in teal, purple and blue. The idea is that my autism doesn't change the world around me, it just shades the way I see it."

Her words resonate so deeply with me. It's like she is describing my whole existence. When I started struggling with my obsessive tendencies, the doctor told my mother that it was just my stress response to having lost everything in the house fire that nearly killed me. Even when they said it, I knew they weren't right. I've been exactly like Ketki describes since I was tiny. I remember sorting my dolls by eye color and hair color. If my little brother messed it up, I would be livid.

Ketki looks crushed. "I knew you'd think it was stupid. Maybe I shouldn't even do it."

"Oh no! You are reading my reaction all wrong. It took

me a while to come up with words to tell you how much it means to me. You just drew a picture of my entire existence."

"I didn't know you were autistic like me."

"Oh, I'm not. I'm just a little shy and awkward. Noise and chaos bother me. I think that's why I like math so much."

Ketki nods sagely. "That's what one of my teachers thought too. Then he got tested for Asperger's syndrome as a grown-up. He was surprised to find out all the things that he thought just made him weird had a medical name."

"That's really interesting. I just thought all these things were personality quirks. I spent a lot of time in the hospital as a kid when I was injured in a house fire. I just thought that made me more shy than most of my friends."

Ketki smiles as she softly says, "I hate to break it to you, but you sound a lot like me and Phoenix."

"What you're saying makes a lot of sense. You guys aren't bad company to keep, for sure. It's a lot to take in. Let me think about it before I decide what to do."

Jade walks over and puts on some bright purple neoprene gloves. "Okay, Ki, I know you've been waiting for this since you were just a kid. I can't believe you're finally old enough to get it done."

"What does your dad say?" I ask, thinking about my mom's reaction when I got my ears pierced on a sleepover.

Ketki raises an eyebrow. "You haven't seen my dad's back, have you?"

"No, I can't say I have. I barely know him, so it would be awkward to ask him to take off his shirt."

Ketki giggles. "Good point. But my dad has a huge

back piece that Jade did years ago. My dad fell in love with my mom right here at Ink'd Deep. It's like the most romantic story ever."

Jade nods. "Even though it was a scary time for Shelby, their love story is pretty epic. Hey, Ketki, you want this on your shoulder, right?"

"I thought about putting it on my back like my dad's, but I want to be able to see it without looking in the mirror. So, can you put it on my left shoulder?"

Jade picks up a marker to draw on Ketki's skin. "You got it. I'm not going to use a stencil for this one. I'm just going to freehand it. I think it works better for the style you want."

"It's hard to trust you because you're going to be poking me thousands of times with the needle. But my dad promises me it won't hurt much."

I can't help but shudder when I think of the pain. "I'm not as brave as you are, Ketki. Needles are not my thing."

"Not to toot my own horn or anything," Jade says as she winks. "But most of the people who hang out with our crew end up getting ink sooner or later. We can start small."

"Umm, I think I'll just watch this time." Just as I say that, my phone buzzes. "Look at that! Saved by the bell." When I look down, I see it's a message from Toby.

Jade looks up from Ketki's tattoo. "Is everything okay?"

"I think so. Toby has located our murder suspect. She just had gallbladder surgery but should be out of the hospital in a few days. I guess we'll go question her then."

"Just be careful," Ketki advises. "I learned the hard way that people who seem to be good are not always who they say they are and people who seem bad may just be misunderstood."

"I think that's especially true in this case. I'll be careful, I promise."

I practically dance in the seat of the rental car. "I can't believe we are doing this! My mom is going to be so surprised! She was upset that I missed her birthday party. So hopefully, this will make it up to her."

Nick smiles. "Well, you know how Tristan is about family. As soon we found out that Shalonda was still in the hospital, and your mom was less than an hour away from where we were headed, he made this happen."

"What about the rest of the team? I feel bad going on a side trip."

"Are you kidding? Toby and Pauline are checking into one of those honeymoon chalets. This is like a gift to them. Neither one of them knows how to take a vacation. So, this is like a bonus honeymoon. Come to think of it, I think Cody was bringing Tori along too. I am sure they'll make good use of the downtime."

"I hope my mom likes you. I haven't really done this meet the parent thing since Thomas. My mom hated him with a passion. Probably for good reason. But it was all kinds of awkward."

"In my experience, parents either love me or hate me. There's really no in between. So, if your mom doesn't like me, it wouldn't be a huge surprise considering how you said your dad treated her. It's gotta be hard for her to trust people."

"What if she does hate you? That would be awful!"

Nick reaches out with his free hand and grabs mine. "If things get off to a rough start, we'll work through it. I can be very charming!"

I smile at his self-deprecating humor. "That's a true statement. I never thought I would get involved with someone I'm working with, yet here you are and we're about to go see my mom. This is all surreal to me."

Nick squeezes my hand. "Relax. After all the family drama we've been through so far, this should be a piece of cake."

My mom serves us all a big piece of peach cobbler with vanilla ice cream. It makes me so homesick. No one cooks like my mom. While waiting to be served dessert, Nick takes a moment to look at the pictures on my mom's old piano. He holds one up and shows it to us. "Allison, is this Sheldon?"

My mom covers her chest as she gasps. "Oh heavens no. I don't have any pictures of that narcissistic monster. Ironically, they burned up in the fire he started. I got this one from my mother-in-law after Dakota and I got settled into a new home. That's Dakota's Grandpa Myron Harper. They were so good to us after the fire. I still can't believe Sheldon was even related to them. God rest their souls."

Nick continues to study the picture intently. "Does Sheldon look like his father?"

"How do the young ones say these days? Sheldon was like Myron's clone."

"Does he still look like this?" Nick presses.

"I don't rightly know. I stopped going to his parole hearings about ten years ago. They were just too hard on Dakota and me. I figured the justice system would make the right decision without involving us."

Nick joins my mom and I at the kitchen table but he doesn't even touch his dessert. After a few moments, he looks at my mom. "I know this is a difficult subject Allison, but do you know where your husband is right now?"

My mom looks at Nick as if he's crazy. "Of course I do! That crazy man is rotting away in prison just like he should be."

Nick grimaces. "I hate to be the bearer of bad news. But I have evidence to suggest that Sheldon Harper has been paroled. He's no longer where you think he is."

"What do you mean?" my mom asks with alarm. "They were supposed to call me if anything happened with his case. After all, we were his victims. We should've been notified!"

My stomach drops. "Mom, did you tell them you moved and got a new phone number?"

My mom smacks her forehead with her palm. "Oh my gosh! I never even thought that. I was just so anxious to start over again. I didn't want any ties to the past."

"Dakota has told you what I usually do for a living, correct?"

"Yeah, she told me you work for some fancy agency that protects movie stars and diplomats."

Nick nods. "I am a bodyguard. Identity Bank is also known for its extensive background checks. Dakota had to undergo one before she could work with the Cold Case Squadron."

I gasp. "They found something on my background check? That's news to me!"

"Not on you specifically, but they did look into your father's whereabouts. He has been paroled."

I close my eyes as the information sinks in. "Are you telling me we've been sitting ducks this whole time?"

Nick shakes his head. "He hadn't been out very long when we discovered his change in status. Tristan, my boss, has placed Josiah with you until we get this sorted."

My mom's jaw goes slack before she asks, "Who's gonna pay for that? You know photography isn't as lucrative as it once was. Everybody has digital cameras on their phones. I don't have that kind of money."

"Don't worry about it. Identity Bank is providing the coverage pro bono. We want to keep you and your daughter safe."

A feeling of dread washes over me. "Nick, are you with me because we have a future or just because I'm some sort of assignment?"

The tips of Nick's ears turn red. "At first, I wanted to know where you were coming from with the whole DNA thing. Then Tristan told me that Sheldon Harper was free. He told me to keep an eye on you. By that time, it wasn't a burden because I was already halfway in love with you."

I feel faint when a thought hits my consciousness. "That old man who's been following me ... is that my dad?"

My mom covers her mouth as she gasps. "You didn't recognize your own father?"

"Something about him struck me as familiar, but I haven't seen him since I was ten. His hair is gray and he has a full beard like Santa Claus."

"Oh dear, that doesn't sound like Sheldon it all. He was always so picky about his personal appearance."

"It is my job to keep your daughter safe, but even if it wasn't, I would still protect her with my life. She means the world to me and I won't let anything happen to either one of you."

My mom wipes away tears. "That makes me so happy. It's clear my daughter adores you. So be careful out there, okay?"

As we drive to the meeting with the Cold Case Squadron team, Nick smiles over at me. "Have you recovered from our meeting with your mom?"

"I can't believe they let my father out of jail without telling either one of us! I know I was only ten when it happened, but I've got scars everywhere to remind myself of what occured. Some kids are scared of monsters that live under the bed. I was scared of the monster I was raised to love. Tell me something —that day we were going to go to the movies, something was wrong, right?"

Nick nods. "There was a car following us even though I made several turns to lose him. I figured the Sweetwater was our safest bet. Their security is pretty tight."

"Why didn't you tell me what was going on back then? If I had known, I wouldn't have gone to the little deli with Jamie."

"Tristan didn't want me to tell you until it was absolutely necessary because he didn't want you to be any more stressed out then you already were. He knows this case is stretching us very thin. So, he made the decision to make sure you were covered even if you guys weren't aware of what was going on."

I pause for a moment to reflect on what Nick just said. Even when I turn it over in my head and try to see his point of view, it doesn't make any sense. "It's almost like you didn't trust my mom and me with the truth and quite honestly that hurts."

Nick squeezes my hand. "It was never about not trusting you. Tristan and I didn't know whether your father would go after either one of you. We were just planning ahead."

"Okay, let's say I buy that argument, after the first incident, you should've told us."

"You're right. I was just hoping I could resolve the issue before it became a real problem."

I let out a frustrated breath. "I thought solving problems together was what we were doing. It sucks to be left out of the loop. Please be honest with me even when you think it's tough."

Nick picks up my hand and kisses my knuckles as we wait at a stop sign. "I can do that. Now, we have to deal with a whole other problem. I'm not looking forward to this meeting with Shalonda."

"Don't worry about it. Pauline and I have a plan. This time, we have you covered."

"Whatever your plan is, I hope it works. Everyone needs answers."

When we discussed our strategy with the profiler, Frank, he decided it would be best if Nick was not present initially.

So, Pauline and I are going to handle this because we've been deemed the least threatening.

Shalonda is already in the room when we enter. I expected her to resemble Cheryl, but I couldn't have been more wrong. Instead, she looks like a fragile, miniature version of me. If she is more than five foot two, I would be amazed.

As she glances around the interrogation room, her hands are trembling. "Why am I here? I paid that stupid parking ticket a long time ago."

Pauline pulls out a chair and sits down. She removes the thick folder from her briefcase. "It's good you paid your parking fine, but that's not why we're here. Before we get started, I have to read you your rights. You have the right to remain silent, anything you say can be used against you in a court of law. If you wish to have an attorney present, one will be appointed for you free of charge."

Shalonda waves Pauline's words away. "Enough of that, tell me what I'm here for. I don't have anything to hide. I'll talk."

I lean forward. "Thanks for coming Ms. Weston. I am Dr. Dakota Crenshaw and this is Detective Pauline Lawrence-Payne. We serve on the Cold Case Squadron. We help solve missing children's cases. We have reason to believe you have information to help solve our case."

"My last name isn't Weston. I went back to my maiden name. It's Jones now. I'm not involved in any missing child case," Shalonda protests.

"Actually, at this point we have discovered that the child in question is not just missing. She was murdered," Pauline replies.

"I don't have any kids. Aren't you listening to me?" Pauline nods. "We are aware. However, your husband is the father of Harmony Hope Scroggins."

"We don't have any kids. We never did. I tried and I couldn't get pregnant."

"That doesn't mean Milo didn't father a child," I gently suggest. "DNA has confirmed Milo was the father of the murdered child. Do you know anything about that?"

Shalonda's eyes dart away from me. "I don't know why you would think I'd know anything."

Pauline scoots her chair closer. "Actually, I do think you know something about what happened to Harmony Hope."

"I don't! I swear," she insists.

Pauline opens the file and pulls out one of Harmony Hope's baby pictures that Cheryl provided "This is your husband's beautiful baby. We know you had knowledge and access to her. In fact, you were probably the last person to ever see this precious baby alive."

Shalonda stubbornly crosses her arms in front of her. "Cute kid, but I don't know anything about her."

"You know, I find that hard to believe since this precious baby was the spitting image of her father. Seems like that's something you would notice."

"I don't know what you're talking about. That kid is a stranger to me. You gotta believe me. I love kids. I wanted to have them more than I wanted to breathe."

Suddenly, my cell phone beeps. Pauline picks up her file and stuffs it in her briefcase, but leaves the picture of

Harmony Hope. "Thank you for your candor. Dr. Crenshaw and I need to return some phone calls. I can have the deputy bring something for you to drink if you'd like."

"Just some water would be fine," Shalonda says as she plays with the cords on her jacket.

"Okay, I'll let the officer know. We'll return shortly."

Pauline motions for me to follow her. As soon as she closes the door, I show her my phone. "This is so weird. It beeped like there was a message, but there isn't anything there."

Pauline stifles a giggle. "That's because I'm the one who pinged you."

"You can do that?" I ask, feeling technology deficient. "I never even saw you send me a text message."

Pauline nods. "I try to give myself an out. I preprogrammed everything into my phone so all I had to do was push a button."

I whistle softly through my teeth. "Wow! You sure know how to make the best use of technology." I point to the room we just left. "So, what's next?"

Pauline grins widely. "We let her stew for a bit. Then we bring in the big guns."

"You gonna let Nick put the fear of God in her?"

Pauline winks. "Pretty much. I hope it makes her move off her lie."

"Honestly, I'm a little worried. The last time Nick confronted a family member, a black eye was involved."

"Nick promised me he would be on his best behavior. We just want to find out the truth. So, if he can help with that, more power to him." Pauline escorts me to a meeting room where Nick is waiting.

He looks so dejected I would like nothing more than to run over and give him a hug. But this is not the time or place. "Hi," I greet shyly.

"So, how is it going in there?" Nick asks.

Pauline shrugs. "Shalonda could be more truthful. So, we need some gentle persuasion."

Nick scrubs his hand down his face. "I was hoping to avoid this confrontation. I sure hope there is such a thing as good karma. If there is, I am earning it in spades."

"No one's arguing any different. I agree with Pauline. I think she's on the verge of telling the truth. She could just use a push," I reply.

Nick grins. "Literally? Because I'd really like to do that."

I shake my head. "Sadly, I just mean a rhetorical push."

"You're always ruining my fun," Nick whines playfully.

"Well, somebody needs to play the grown-up."

"Yeah, I'm not going to comment. So, you guys just need me to be menacing?"

Pauline nods. "How about we just play it by ear? I don't think it's going to take very much for her to crack."

Nick shrugs. "I can do that. Let's go get justice for Harmony Hope." Nick places his hand at the small of my waist as we walk down the hall to the interview room.

Pauline pastes a smile on her face as she greets Shalonda. "Sorry that took so long. We had to consult with another member of the Cold Case Squadron."

Pauline steps aside to reveal Nick. I watch Shalonda's reaction closely. She seems to sway in her seat as she turns pale.

"What is he doing here?" she demands. "Is Milo here too?" She tries to look out into the hallway to see if anyone else is coming.

"It's good to see you too, Shalonda. Although I never expected to be talking to my sister-in-law under conditions like this," Nick subtly taunts.

"I don't know why they think I'm a suspect! You know me. I could never hurt anybody. Remember, I used to even take the spiders out of the house instead of squishing them."

Nick nods. "That may be true. But, you didn't have a grudge against critters and bugs. I suspect you felt a lot more anger toward the woman who was sleeping with your husband. It must have been difficult to watch Cheryl be able to accomplish what you couldn't."

"How dare you!" she seethes. Just like that, it's like a switch was flipped. The fragile meek woman suddenly turns into an angry banshee. "Why should he be able to have a child with some common street urchin?"

"Who are you referring to?" Pauline asks.

"That dip wad, Milo, got tired of waiting for me to get pregnant. So he went and slept with his brother's fiancée. He thought he was being so sneaky. But his whore was always visiting her grandma right across the street from our house. I saw Milo canoodling with her and sure enough, I could see with my own eyes she was having a baby. So, I decided she didn't deserve to be pregnant. I tried to run her down when she was riding a bicycle but she was too quick for me. So, I decided I would kill her and take the baby."

Nick puts his hands up in a timeout gesture. "Wait, I'm confused. Cheryl Scoggins is still alive and Harmony Hope is dead. So, what happened?"

"I don't know what happened to that whore – I refuse to call her by her name — but whatever happened to her, she started getting really paranoid and looking over her shoulder. Maybe it was because I tried to run her over with the car, but anyway I couldn't get close enough to hurt her."

I swallow hard before I ask, "So you decided to hurt the baby instead?"

"No! I was going to adopt her. I even had a special christening dress made for her. As far as I knew that whore didn't have any family to help her raise the child. So, if she was out of the way Milo and I could adopt his daughter and I would still be a mother."

I'm reeling from her disclosure. I can't imagine just deciding I want someone else's child to raise as my own.

Pauline points to the picture she had given Shalonda "Tell me how your plan goes from killing Cheryl Scoggins to murdering Harmony Hope?"

"Well I couldn't believe my luck one day when Cheryl put a note in our mailbox telling me my child had arrived more than a year before. She obviously wanted me to take the baby otherwise she would have never told Milo and left the baby with her senile old grandmother. That woman barely knew her name. She couldn't take care of the baby. So, I went over there and got her."

"Then what," I blurt as curiosity overtakes me.

"Well that little brat was so ungrateful. I showed her all the toys I bought her and even got her a new stuffed bear because hers was just nasty. She wasn't thankful it all. She kept bawling for her mama. It didn't matter what I did, she just wanted that other woman. So, she wouldn't stop crying. I made her shut up."

"What did you do?" Nick asks with trepidation.

"I sat on that little brat until she shut up. Then, I was going to put her in her crib and show Milo what a good mom I could be. But she started turning blue. That's when I figured maybe I sat on her too long. I put some duct tape around her face and her arms and legs. I was hoping if anybody found her, they would think she was kidnapped by someone who didn't know her. You know, like they do on all those television crime shows."

"I can't believe this. How could you be so cold?" Nick mutters under his breath.

Pauline ignores Nick's comment as she presses ahead. "How did you dispose of her body when you discovered she was dead?"

Shalonda looks proud of herself as she explains, "I used to work on a janitorial crew to make some extra money. You know, we cleaned offices. I knew this guy who raises cattle. He had a bunch of wells on his property. I figured she was tiny and would fit in the opening. So, I dressed her in the new christening dress and put her there. I never thought anyone would find her."

"Cheryl says she got a letter stating Harmony Hope was being kept safe. Where did that letter come from?"

Shalonda puffs up a little. "I wrote that letter! The whore was too stupid to believe it came from anyone other than her lover. I wanted to make sure she didn't call the police before Milo and I could settle down in a new place with Harmony Hope."

Abruptly, Pauline stands up and pulls a set of handcuffs from her waistband. "Shalonda Jones, you are under arrest for the murder of Harmony Hope Scroggins."

"This is not fair! I should've been her mother, not that whore. At least that little baby is in heaven now instead of being with that lying, cheating witch. I'm not even sorry! That woman didn't deserve to be a mother."

After a local police officer escorts Shalonda out of the interrogation room, Pauline sinks back in her chair and lets out a deep breath. "Boy, it's a good thing we didn't turn off the tape recorder as soon as the interview was over. That confession may just wrap the whole thing up."

"Maybe so, but that doesn't mean there aren't going to be a whole lot of broken hearts along the way."

Pauline looks at Nick somberly. "I've known you for a really long time. I've never seen you this unhappy. Don't let your hearts be the ones broken in this case. Love really can triumph over all. Don't lose hope."

Nick heaves a gigantic sigh. "Why does everyone keep saying that? This is the most hopeless situation I've ever been in."

Pauline smiles softly. "I know this is tough. Sometimes, you just have to look for the silver lining. Think of it this way. Shalonda won't be able to hurt anyone else."

# Chapter Twenty-Two

## Nick

I take a spring roll and put it on Dakota's plate. "I hope you don't mind that we didn't go out to eat. I don't think I'm up to facing people right now."

"Don't worry about it," she says as she takes the plate from me. "Today was unusually brutal."

I set the takeout container down on the table and rub my temples. "Brutal is one word for it. I didn't expect it to be quite so hard since I already knew it was likely Shalonda was guilty. Somehow hearing her brag about it like it was her only option was enough to undo me."

"I know. I just can't get over her faulty logic. Just because Milo screwed up doesn't mean Harmony Hope needed to die. I don't know how she made that connection in her brain."

"Obviously, there is something wrong with her brain. No sane person would think that way. Now I need to figure out a way to tell my brother and Cheryl."

Dakota comes over and hugs me from behind. "You don't have to do that. I'm part of the Cold Case Squadron. I could make the notifications for you. There's no need for you to put yourself through any more pain."

I shake my head. "I appreciate it, but I owe it to my family to tell them personally. I mean, I know Cheryl wasn't technically family but she's been in my life long enough I owe her the same respect."

She walks over and grabs her computer from the side table. "Okay, I understand. But if you're going to do it, we might as well do it together."

"Okay, give me a minute to collect my thoughts as we eat. I just don't know how much to share."

"I know it's hard. Even so, I think they would appreciate the most honest answer you can give — even if it contains disturbing details. When I was recovering from my burns, I could always tell when people weren't being honest. It made me more scared than I would've been if they had just told me the truth. That's why it was so tough on me when you didn't tell me about my father being paroled. Just make sure you tell the whole truth."

"I know that's probably the best approach. But I'm still at a loss of how to explain Shalonda's actions."

"Anybody would be. Her behavior doesn't follow any logic and her actions are not the actions of someone who is mentally well."

"I really wish I knew whether Shalonda was sick or just a purely evil person. It would make this so much easier to understand."

"This will all come out at trial — unless she takes a plea."

My eyes widen. "You think she might actually get away with it?"

"I didn't say that. I'm just saying a smart attorney

might consider a plea deal, given her confession and the fact that she said she was happy that she killed Harmony Hope. Pauline played it by the book and there doesn't seem to be very much wiggle room. She already gleefully told us she was guilty."

Dakota brings her food to the breakfast bar where I've been sitting. Together, we eat in silence as I try to gather my thoughts and decide what to tell everyone about my horrific day. Dakota is right. I don't do anyone a service if I don't tell them the whole truth, even if it hurts.

Finally, I put my fork down and turn to Dakota. "Come on, let's do this. It's not going to get any easier if I wait. I just wish there was a way to tell them both at once. I don't want to have to repeat the garbage we heard today."

Dakota points to her laptop. "Toby, Phoenix and I have been videoconferencing. So Toby put teleconferencing software on the computer for me. We should be able to put Cheryl and Milo on the same conference call. That way, you'd only have to tell the whole morbid story once."

"Actually, I'm going to have to tell it twice, whether I want to or not. My mom deserves to be told this kind of news in person."

Dakota grimaces. "Yeah, you're right. This isn't the kind of thing you want to spring on someone if they don't know it's coming. Do you want me to dial their numbers? I have them in a database on my computer."

I sigh deeply. "Go ahead. We might as well get started."

I don't know how Dakota did it, but my brother and Cheryl come online at the same time. "This can't be good," Milo says when he sees us.

I suck in a deep breath and let it out. "It's not good. I

can't sugarcoat it. We talked to Shalonda today. She confessed to everything. She was trying to make you pay for your affair with Cheryl. If she couldn't have any kids, she didn't want Cheryl to have any of your children either."

"She killed my daughter because she was jealous?" Cheryl asks.

Dakota comes into frame. "It would seem so. What we don't know is whether she is truly mentally ill or evil.

"At this point, does it really matter? Our daughter is dead and nothing is going to bring her back. So, kudos to her for confessing to what we all figured out she'd already done. I hope she rots in hell!"

I can see Milo close his eyes in anguish "I understand why you would feel that way. I just can't reconcile the person you're describing with who I was in love with for a decade. I don't understand. If she loves kids so much, why did she kill my daughter?"

Dakota shakes her head. "Don't do that to yourselves. You can't figure out what makes a mad person tick. It just is what it is. I'm sorry your daughter got caught up in the madness. But it's not your fault!"

Cheryl sobs. "It feels like it was my fault. I knew my MawMaw wasn't well. I just felt like I didn't have any other options. And now my child is gone from my life forever."

Milo clears his throat. "Cheryl, I owe you an apology. I should have believed you the first time you mentioned Harmony Hope. If I had, none of this would have happened."

Dakota replies, "I know it's tempting to feel like you're responsible for what happened. But you're not. You can't rationalize the acts of a madwoman. Both of you had no idea what you were dealing with."

"She was my wife! I should've known the pressure was getting to her. I never should have hooked up with Cheryl."

"At least we can both agree on that," Cheryl says wryly. "Nick, while we're apologizing, I need to say I'm sorry for doing this to you too."

"Ditto for me, brother. So, what do we do now?"

I let out a deep sigh. "The only thing we can do to honor Harmony is to make sure Shalonda goes to jail. She's been arrested. Her confession will do a lot to help the district attorney. I suspect we'll all have to testify eventually."

"Gladly!" Milo replies emphatically. "I may have loved Shalonda for years, but that doesn't excuse what she did."

Cheryl lets out a sob. "I can't talk about this anymore. Thanks for letting me know." She signs off the call and her screen goes blank.

I study my brother carefully. "Will you be okay?"

"Not today. Maybe not ever. I can't believe how devastated I am over losing a child I never even met. But that's where I am at. I didn't even get a chance to say hello, let alone goodbye."

"I'm so sorry. I wish there was something I could do to make it better."

Dakota pushes her hair out of her eyes and tucks it behind her ear before she leans forward and into the camera range. "It won't change the past, but it might help if you had an opportunity to say goodbye to your daughter. She is buried in Owl Creek, Tennessee. Maybe a small memorial service would help everyone come to terms with the loss."

Milo hangs his head. "We should've been celebrating

birthdays, Father's Day, Christmas and lost teeth. A funeral is not the way I wanted to remember my daughter. But, I think you're right. We need to remember her somehow."

"Okay, I'm going to let Mom know what's going on. Do you want to be part of that?

"Please tell me you are not planning to do this over the phone. Somebody needs to be with her when she finds out that her granddaughter was murdered."

"I totally agree. Dakota and I are flying out to see her in the morning. If you want to be part of it, let me know."

Milo shakes his head. "This may be cowardly of me, but I don't think I can handle a showdown with Mom right now. She is going to be so disappointed in me. I can't deal with one more heartbreak."

My brother looks so devastated I wish I could reach through the video screen and give him a hug. I know we've had our differences in the past and I still don't understand his decision to cheat with the woman he knew I loved, but no one deserves to have their child murdered.

I wipe away a tear. "Don't worry. We'll take care of mom."

"I'll be in touch about a funeral service," Dakota adds. "Please be gentle with yourself."

Milo wipes tears away with the back of his hands. "Thanks for everything. Tell Mom I love her, and I'm so sorry for what happened."

"That goes without saying."

As we walk up the steps of my family home, Dakota pauses

on the step above me. She turns around and kisses me gently. "I know this is going to be tough. Just know regardless of what happens, I'm in your corner."

I place my arms around her waist and pull her close. "You have no idea what that means to me." I take a deep breath before I say, "Let's do this."

As I say that, my mom's front door swings wide open. "Nicholas Weston, what are you doing here? I thought you were working in Florida."

"I am, Mom. Today, my job brings me back home."

My mom fans away tears with her hand. "This has something to do with all those strange questions you were asking me about our family, doesn't it — that little girl who you said was our kinfolk?"

Dakota grips my hand. "You mind if we come in, Mrs. Weston? It will take a while for Nick and me to explain what's going on."

My mom steps aside. "I have a bad feeling about this," she murmurs under her breath.

Mentally, I agree. There is nothing good about what's going on. However, I try to keep my expression neutral as my mom escorts us in the house and offers us some sweet tea.

I thank her and take a long sip before I start to explain, "Remember when we told you that Dakota was looking into our family to help solve a murder?"

"Of course I do! I've been racking my brain trying to figure out who could possibly be involved. I couldn't come up with anybody."

"Mom, there is no easy way to say this. But, Dakota and I have solved the mystery with the help of the Cold

Case Squadron."

"You figured out who that poor little girl belongs to?"

When I pause to collect my thoughts I look over at Dakota in a panic. I honestly don't know what to say. The next words out of my mouth are going to crush my mother. Seeing my distress, Dakota jumps in to answer the question.

"Yes ma'am, we did. Initially, DNA analysis put the focus on your family. Even though the victim's DNA was degraded, we were able to eliminate Nick as the source of the DNA, however his DNA test underscored the fact that Baby Jane Doe was a member of your family."

"I already told you I only have two sons and neither of them are fathers. Their cousins are all dead. So, how could this be true?"

I reach across the table and grasped my mother's hands. "Mom, Baby Jane Doe is actually Harmony Hope Scroggins."

My mom gasps and puts her hand over her heart. "You had a baby with Cheryl? Why didn't you say something?"

"Sadly, Harmony Hope was not my daughter. She was my niece."

"What was your brother doing sleeping with your girlfriend?"

"That's a really good question. There doesn't seem to be an acceptable answer. Milo said he was having problems in his marriage to Shalonda and Cheryl claimed she did it to make me jealous."

"Are you sure about this? This story sounds like something from one of my daytime soaps."

Dakota nods. "I'm sorry Mrs. Weston. DNA tests have

confirmed that Milo and Cheryl were the parents of Harmony Hope."

"Oh, my poor grandbaby!" My mom wails before collapsing back against the chair. "What happened to her?"

"As nearly as we can tell, Cheryl left her daughter with Helen Scroggins."

My mom turns pale. "What? Cheryl's grandmother was more than a few cards shy of a full deck."

"Maybe so, but for personal reasons, Cheryl figured she didn't have any choice but to leave Harmony there," Dakota replies.

"Did Helen Scroggins murder my grandchild?" my mom demands.

I scrub my hands down my face before I disclose, "No, there's no evidence Helen hurt the baby. It turns out the true culprit is Shalonda."

"My daughter-in-law killed another woman's baby?"

Dakota nods. "It would appear so. She confessed to murdering Harmony so that another woman wouldn't have the option of being her mother."

My mom shakes her head. "I just can't believe it. That's the craziest thing I have ever heard. Now, I always thought Shalonda was a little bit odd. But I never thought she would hurt someone — especially, a child."

Dakota heaves a heavy sigh. "I know it seems unlikely, but all of the evidence fits. To confirm this, we had a note Shalonda gave to Cheryl analyzed for a handwriting match. So, not only does the DNA lineup with Cheryl and Milo, the handwriting match shows that Shalonda wrote the note to Cheryl to assure her that Harmony was being properly cared for."

"Properly cared for — my butt. A beautiful child of God is dead now. That's hardly proper."

"Fortunately, law enforcement agrees with us. Shalonda is in custody until the trial."

"Well, thank God for small miracles," my mom says with a huff.

After a couple of beats of silence, my mom asks, "How is your brother handling this?"

I press my lips together in a thin line. "Last I checked, Milo was having a hard time processing everything. He feels compelled to blame himself."

"As well he should," my mom spits. "If you're going to make an idiotic move like that, you have to be prepared for the consequences."

"I agree that the affair wasn't Milo's finest move. But, he is devastated at the outcome."

"He should be. Cheryl was your girlfriend. He should've kept his hands to himself."

The lips of my mouth turn up. "I don't disagree with you mom, but I forgive Milo for what happened. We can all have lapses in personal judgment. That's what this was."

My mom just shakes her head. "You are far more forgiving than I could ever be. This should outrage you."

I smiled gently. "It does, Mom — but I haven't had a chance to let it all sink in yet. I'm sure when it does, I'll be devastated. But right now, we're just trying to make sure Shalonda is brought to justice."

"What about the poor little girl who is dead? What are we going to do about that?"

Dakota smiles at my mom. "The town of Owl Creek

has adopted your granddaughter as their own. So, she is buried in a quaint little cemetery. Nick and I are planning a memorial service for the little girl we never got the chance to know. Hopefully, you can join us and get a sense of peace about it all."

Thea puts her head in her hands. "All my friends are bragging about their grandkids. Now, I get to explain why I don't have one. I'm not sure I'm prepared to deal with that."

Dakota nods her head. "I understand. After my burns, everyone knew who I was because my burn case had garnered so much media attention. It was hard to relive my experience as I disclosed my past to friends and family — and eventually the whole world."

"Oh you poor thing, how did you cope with all that?"

"In the beginning, honestly I didn't cope very well. Now, I put it all into perspective and placed it as far out of my mind as I possibly can. I've got new hopes, dreams and aspirations to follow next to the man who sees all the way down to my soul and helps me find hope."

"That's so sweet!" my mom exclaims.

Dakota blushes. "No, it's true. I wasn't looking for love. Love found me in the arms of your son. It's a great place to be. I've never felt so unconditionally accepted in my whole life. You raised wonderful sons."

My mom looks at me with adoration. "Yeah, I suppose I did. Even if one of them was a knucklehead. So, what's gonna happen with that poor, sweet child?"

I clear my throat as emotion overtakes me. "Well, we were planning a small memorial service to say our goodbyes."

"A grandmother should never have to meet her

grandchild this way," my mom protests.

I stand up, walk over and give my mom a tight hug. "I agree, Mom. I totally agree."

It took only a week to get everything organized, thanks to Tristan's organizing acumen. It's as if God is smiling down on us. It is a beautiful July day in Owl Creek, Tennessee. Dakota is looking regal in her simple long sleeved black dress and low heeled shoes. She reminds me of Grace Kelly.

I'm in shirtsleeves because I couldn't handle a jacket on a day like today. The minister hasn't even started yet and my mom is crying softly at the edge of Baby Jane Doe's plot. I don't know how Tristan pulled it off, but beside Baby Jane Doe's granite marker, there is a new headstone with an etched teddy bear identifying the remains as Harmony Hope Scroggins.

Out of the corner of my eye, I see Cheryl go up to my mom. Reluctantly, my mom hugs her and starts to weep.

Pastor Walter Walters stands behind the small granite marker. He clears his throat loudly. "May I have your attention please?"

As if by magic, everyone stops talking and faces Walter. Walter holds up a portrait of Harmony Hope. "I can't say I knew this precious little soul. I wish I had because every child is a child of God. This particular baby was taken far too soon under circumstances we don't even want to ponder."

Cheryl's knees suddenly buckle and Milo reaches out to catch her.

The minister waits for Cheryl to compose herself before he continues. "The circumstances under which Harmony Hope came into the world matter not. Harmony Hope is still a beloved child of God. Most of us here didn't get a chance to know and love this child." He looks directly at Cheryl before continuing. "But for those of you who did adore this baby, my prayers are especially with you."

He sets the portrait down on top of the new headstone and bows his head. "Heavenly Father, we ask that you give us grace and healing as we mourn the loss of a child who is gone too soon. May she receive a measure of justice and know she was forever loved. In Jesus name we pray, Amen."

We all murmur amen, and my mom goes over to Milo and Cheryl to give them a huge hug.

"We all make mistakes in our lives, the secret is to learn from them and become better people. I'm so sorry it had to happen this way. But sometimes God does things we don't understand. But, don't you go blaming yourselves for something a crazy woman did. As awful as this was, it's not your fault."

"I appreciate your kind words, Mrs. Weston. I just can't help wishing I would've done things differently," Cheryl says as she looks directly at me.

"I understand, child. I think we all feel that way from time to time. But, unfortunately we can't turn back the hands of time."

# CHAPTER TWENTY-THREE

# DAKOTA

As I'm completing paperwork to document the Cold Case Squadron's findings, my phone rings. Absently, I pick it up.

"Hello?"

"Dakota, is that you?"

"Hey Mom, what's up?"

"I went grocery shopping today. There was a guy following me. I don't think it's your dad. This was a younger guy. He looks a little bit like a model. Do you think it's that Josiah guy?"

"Probably so. Did he make any aggressive moves toward you?"

"Oh heavens no. I could just tell out of the corner of my eye he was keeping watch. When I left, he left too. His SUV is parked a couple houses down."

"Mom, it's probably just the bodyguard assigned to you. If you'd like, I can check with Tristan just to make sure."

"Oh could you please? This whole thing about your father has me completely spooked. I'm afraid to leave my house to check my mail. Your father almost killed all of us. I don't think he's gonna stop until he succeeds."

"I know. I've been having nightmares since Nick told us Sheldon was free."

"I can't believe they let him out of prison. Maybe I should have fought harder to keep him there. I just thought our stories were powerful enough to keep him out of society."

"I struggle with that too. I don't know if we could've made a difference or not."

"Are you staying safe? I worry about you being so far away."

"We are good, Mom. Nick is taking really good care of me. I'm just doing some paperwork today and tomorrow we are going to go to a friend's wedding."

"Please be careful. I don't want anything awful to happen to you. Your dad is a vengeful man. I think we should both remember that."

I reach over my shoulder and trace a prominent scar. "Trust me, I've never ever forgotten what kind of man

Sheldon Harper is. I'll remember until the day I die. I'll call Tristan to double check whether you should be worried about someone following you. Call you right back."

After I hang up with my mother, I call Tristan. "Hey Tristan, sorry to bother you but I have a question."

"Let me guess, you're worried about what to wear to Dylan's wedding?"

"No, Lauren already warned me to wear pants because it's supposed to be a little chilly on the beach. I actually called to check on something else."

"Shoot, I'm all ears."

"Umm … This is going to sound silly but Nick told me everything he knew about my dad. So, my mom is worried because she saw someone following her but I told her not to worry because I figured it was one of your guys. Do you have someone covering my mom?"

"Affirmative. I assigned Josiah to your mother as soon as we found out the threat was legitimate. Josiah's one of my most skilled assets. In addition to being a fine bodyguard, he is a phenomenal medic."

"Does that mean you expect something awful to happen to my mother?"

"Not exactly, but in this business it never hurts to be overly cautious."

"Okay, I can see that. I'll let my mom know that the person she saw is likely Josiah. I have one more question for you. Do you think Nick is only sticking around because I'm his protection assignment?"

Tristan chuckles, "I've seen Nick perform in a variety of high pressure situations. He has worked hundreds of cases for me over the last few years. I've never seen him so personally invested. I think he's sticking around because he likes you. Otherwise, your interactions would've been quite formal."

"Formal isn't quite the word I would associate with Nick," I admit.

"Exactly! Be sure that Nick is looking out for you every hour of every day, but beyond that, he enjoys spending time with you."

"Thanks for the reassurance. We'll see you tomorrow at the wedding."

"You're welcome. If it makes you feel better, I can assure you that Nick is exactly where he wants to be."

"I can see why Lauren asked us to wear pants today. It's windy out here." I comment as I brace myself against another strong gust of wind.

Nick moves behind me and puts his arms around my waist to help protect me from the wind. "Yeah, this weather is throwing everything out of whack. But this beach has sentimental value to Dylan and Lauren. This is where they fell in love."

"Aww, that sounds like something from the movies. If someone asked me where I fell in love with you, I'm not sure I can answer that."

Nick gives me a smug smile. "That's an easy one. I fell in love with you at Ketki's impromptu dance party. That's when I knew I couldn't imagine my life without you."

I spin around and look him directly in the eye. "Seriously? That was so early! We barely knew each other back then."

Nick nods. "I know. But that didn't matter to me. Being around you made me believe in the power of love again."

Dylan comes up behind Nick and taps him on the shoulder. "Careful what you say, buddy. Your love story could overshadow my big day."

Nick clamped his mouth shut before he says, "Geez, I'm sorry. I guess I got carried away."

Dylan laughs out loud. "I see you left your humor in your other pants too. I am teasing. You know this group rejoices any time someone falls in love. It couldn't have happened to a nicer guy. I am sorry things turned out the way they did with your family, but I have to say you found a heckuva silver lining."

"I did. I am thrilled we met. I'm just sorry about the circumstances."

Dylan nods. "I get it, I really do. I felt the same way while I was falling in love with Lauren. I'm here to tell you love can conquer anything."

Suddenly, music plays from the speakers strategically placed on the beach.

Dylan glances down at his dress watch. "That's my cue. I've got to go. Thanks for coming today."

After he leaves, I thread my fingers through Nick's. "That right there is what gives me hope we are going to work out."

"Yeah, their meeting was almost as crazy as ours. They seem to be handling it well."

Nick and I make our way to the seats on the beach as a dog wearing a bow somberly walks up the aisle to a chorus of awws. After a stunning young woman walks the dog up the aisle, she stands next to Dylan. The dog takes a seat in front of the rows of chairs. Next, Pauline and Toby walk up the aisle followed by Cody and Tori. Cody grins at Dylan standing by the minister. He walks up and gives him a fist bump. "It's about time you guys finally tied the knot. You've been engaged forever."

"Well, some of us have more patience than others," Dylan answers with a grin. He laughed out loud when he realizes his words have been caught on the microphone.

Declan starts playing the wedding march on his guitar while Jade holds a microphone in front of it. Out of the corner of my eye, I see Dylan tear up when he spots his fiancée. Lauren is wearing a simple white halter dress with a small train. As she's walking up the aisle, her veil is whipping around so violently in the wind, I'm afraid it's going to shred before the ceremony is over.

The same minister who delivered the eulogy and prayer at Harmony Hope's funeral taps the microphone. "Can everyone hear me? I can't say I've ever performed a wedding right on the beach. This is a new experience for me. But, you know this group — they specialize in the unusual. If you don't know me, I'm Jessica's grandpa. I started my ministry in Kansas, but I must say the weather is better here in Florida, even if we're about to blow away."

Jessica clears her throat. "Grandpa, it's cold out here. You might want to move it along."

"You're right, Buttercup, I should get this show on the road. Ladies and gentlemen, who gives this woman to be married?

A woman I presume to be Lauren's mom steps forward. "I do. Without this man, I would not have had a relationship with my daughter. If Lauren's father were here, he would give his enthusiastic blessing. You are exactly the type of man Devon always hoped his daughter would grow up and marry. Therefore, with great pleasure I give my consent for her to be married."

Dylan whispers, "Thanks for the vote of confidence Janita. I will do my best to keep your daughter safe."

Lauren dabs at her eyes with a tissue. "I love you, Mom. I'm glad you came around to cherish Dylan too."

"You picked a good one, for sure," Janita says as she pats Dylan on the shoulder on the way back to her seat.

Even Pastor Walters is wiping away tears before he says, "Lauren, I understand you have some things to say to your beloved, Dylan."

Lauren reaches in her pocket and draws out a piece of paper. I nudge Nick and mouth, "Look, it has pockets." He grins and gives me a thumbs up.

Lauren's hands shake as she meticulously straightens the piece of paper out before she starts to read.

If I were in Dylan's shoes, I would be a nervous wreck. But he is simply standing there waiting for her to collect herself. He breathes in and out almost as if in slow motion. She mimics his breaths.

Finally, she looks up and smiles. "This is why I need you in my life. You help me breathe even when it's hard. You saw past my panic attacks to see who I really was. You came into my world to help me find my big sister. Sadly, you found that April had been killed by a psychopath. This was not the outcome we were hoping for, of course."

Dylan whispers, "You'll never know how much I wished I could bring April back to you alive."

Lauren steps forward to give Dylan a comforting hug. "Oh, I know. It was written all over your face and encoded in everything you did for me and my mom. I know it was hard on you as a detective." She steps back and grasps his hands. "Yet, you were beside me every step of the journey and you've never left even when times got tough. For those reasons and so many others, Dylan Palmer I love you and can't wait to be your wife."

The pastor clears his throat as he takes a bright red hanky out of his pocket and dabs at his eyes. "That was beautiful, Lauren. Dylan that's a tough one to follow, but would you like to try?"

Dylan grins at Pastor Walters. "It's always tough to follow Lauren. She's just that phenomenal. I want this woman and everyone here to know how much she changed my life. Oh, I was putting on a really great show before I met Lauren Drysdale. I was there to help put her family back together, but in reality Lauren gave me permission to look at the world without the prism of my job. She helped me find balance in this crazy world while still being true to who I was. May I always live up to the hero she sees when she looks at me. For those reasons and so many others, I, Dylan Palmer, love you more than life itself and can't wait to be your husband."

"I understand the two of you have rings to signify your love story," Pastor Walters says as he gestures toward them.

Lauren digs in her pocket. When she opens her hand, there are two rings laying on her palm. She blushes. "I couldn't decide which kind of ring to get you, so I got you both. This first ring is my father's wedding ring. Before that, it belonged to my dad's grandfather. So, since my dad isn't here to welcome you into the family, the ring will have to suffice."

Dylan holds out his hand for her to place the ring on. After she finishes, she holds up the other ring. "I love you so much I want to make sure you stay as safe as possible. So, when you're not being fancy, you can wear this silicone ring at work or when you're working out. I love every part of you and I don't want you to lose a finger just because you want to wear a wedding ring."

Nick puts his arm around my shoulder and I lean my head on his chest. "That's darn thoughtful of her," he whispers.

Dylan grins. "Yet another example of the thousands of ways you take care of me every day. I am such a lucky guy."

Pastor Walters looks at Dylan. "Your turn, Mr.

Palmer."

Dylan turns toward the audience. "Just for the record, I know I'm never going to top what Lauren just did for me. But, this is my attempt to remind her every day how much I love her. I'm sure you guys will all see this at the reception, but I had this ring handcrafted with tiny sea shells and star fish to remind her of the first date we ever went on. I think I fell in love that day and I've grown to be more in love with her every day since." Dylan turns to Lauren and declares "I hope you never doubt how much you've changed my life for the better. I love you, Lauren."

I watch Lauren's hand tremble as Dylan gently places the shiny silver ring on her ring finger. Lauren has her eyes closed while he puts on the ring. After he's finished, she opens her eyes and gasps. "It's like you pulled this out of my imagination. I can't imagine anything more perfect. I love you too, Dylan."

"By exchanging these rings you acknowledge that you promise to love, support, and cherish each other until death parts you. Like these rings, true love has no beginning or end. It goes on forever."

Lauren and Dylan turned to the pastor with their hands intertwined. "We do."

"By the power vested in me in the states of Kentucky, Virginia, and Florida, I hereby pronounce you man and wife." Pastor Walters winks at the audience before continuing, "Just remember, you're setting the stage for the rest of your life, right here and now. Don't screw it up."

Dylan gives a startled laugh. "Okay, no pressure here."

Dylan scoops Lauren up in his arms as if she weighs nothing. He leans down and tenderly kisses her. When he is done, he looks up and exclaims, "If that's the way married life is going to treat me, I'm glad I signed up."

I lift my foot up and check for blisters. "That was fun, but I have to stop if I want to be able to walk tomorrow. Have I mentioned how much I love dancing with you?"

"Yeah, we've got a good thing going."

"You have no idea. Usually I'm not in sync with my partners like I am with you. That can get painful after a while."

I sit down at the table in the bar Tristan rented out for the reception. I flex my feet and take a sip of iced tea. Nick feeds me a piece of cake. "This is the life, I could get used to something like this. You all spoil me too much."

Nick tucks a stray strand of hair behind my ear. "It's not spoiling if it's what you deserve."

I sigh wistfully. "It was such a beautiful wedding from the invitations all the way through to the cake. It was like a fairytale except I was living it with Dylan and Lauren. Even Sara Lee was perfectly behaved. I couldn't believe Lauren taught her how to dance so they could play a prank on Dylan during the first dance. That was the most amazing thing I've ever seen in my life."

"Yeah, that was phenomenal. You know, I could see us having something like that at our wedding with Mr. Pawsome."

I'm so shocked at his statement I don't know what to say. I can't come up with any words which make sense.

Nick must have read my expression. "What?"

"I didn't know you were thinking about us in those

terms." Red-faced, I admit, "I mean I hoped we were on the same page, but you never know.

"We've been almost inseparable since the first time we met. I haven't so much as thought of another woman since you came into my life. I guess I just thought you knew how I felt. So, yeah, I think about us in terms of old ranch houses with big front porches, rocking chairs and grandkids. I see us getting a puppy to play with Mr. Pawsome. I love you and I don't want to be with anyone else. Ever."

My eyes mist up. "I fell in love with you a long time ago, but our lives are so different and we live in different states. I was afraid to hope you felt the same way as me. I still don't know how were going to solve the logistics. After being here with you, I'm not sure a long distance relationship is going to be enough."

"I feel the same way. You have a great job and so do I. We just have to figure out how to make those jobs compatible with love."

# Chapter Twenty-Four

## Nick

Even as I assure Dakota how much I love her and emphasize the fact that I've never been so serious in my life, I don't think she fully understands where I'm coming from.

Dakota is watching me carefully through tear stained eyes. Although I had planned this differently, I know what I need to do to convince her.

Dropping down to one knee, I fish a little packet out of my pocket. I've been carrying it around for weeks, waiting for the perfect time. I guess there is no time like the present.

Dakota's eyes widened as she watches me remove a ring from the tissue paper. "Is this what I think it is?"

"Do you want it to be?" I ask, dreading her answer.

She pauses for a moment. "I think I do."

"Dakota Hope Crenshaw, I love you more than I ever thought possible. Will you marry me?"

A tear trickles down her face as she looks at me somberly. "I wish I could, but if I say yes, one of us has to give up our careers. We've both worked hard to get where we are. It's not fair for us to move forward before this case is solved. I can't ask you to choose between loyalty to your family and me. I've thought about this a million times, I just don't know how we can be truly happy with all this hanging over our heads."

I didn't realize I was holding my breath until my lungs starts to burn. Reluctantly, I qualify my proposal. "Okay, don't answer me right now. Let me figure out all the glitches so you can say yes with one hundred percent of your heart and your mind."

She slips off her shoes and launches herself into my arms. "Thank you so much for not brushing off my fears. I love you and I want to make this work. But I came here to solve a case. I can't just leave that undone. Whatever happens, I don't want us to sacrifice who we are so we can love the other person."

"I'm pretty good at solving problems. So stay tuned."

I put my arm around her waist and escort her to a quiet corner of the dance floor and tuck her under my chin as a slow ballad plays. "I love Kenny Rogers, how did you know this is my favorite song?" she asks.

"Lucky guess or divine intervention. I don't know which. I just want you to know I'll be working on a solution until I find one. Life without you is not an option for me."

She stands on her tiptoes and kisses my chin. "Just for the record, what happened here tonight is not a 'no'. It's a 'Let's figure it all out before we jump in with both feet.' I love you and I'm praying we can work everything out. We've been through so much. It would be a shame to give up now."

"Consider your self warned. I tend to go after what I

want in life — and I want you. I'll move heaven and earth to make you happy."

Dakota wraps her arms around my waist and hugs me tightly. "I know. That's why I love you so much."

Tristan comes into the break room as I am heating some Swedish meatballs and egg noodles.

"Well, Weston, I think your lunch smells better than mine." He sniffs the air and smiles.

"I wish I could take credit for it, but I can't. Dakota made this dish last night for dinner. I thought it was pretty impressive, considering how small the kitchenette is in her hotel suite."

"I know the feeling. When Rogue and I first got together, she had this dilapidated apartment. Her stove only had one working burner, yet she could turn out some of the best food I've ever eaten. I bet Dakota is looking forward to going home. As nice as the Sweetwater is, it's not the same as being in your own surroundings."

I sigh. "Dakota may be looking forward to going home, but I'd be a happy guy if she could stay here."

Tristan grins at me. "So it's like that?"

"Yeah, it has been for a while. I went out on a limb and asked her to marry me. I didn't get the response I was expecting."

Tristan's expression is comical as his jaw drops open. "Dakota said no? Get out of town!"

I shake my head. "She didn't say no, but she didn't exactly say yes either. She doesn't see a way forward for us even though we love each other very much. She doesn't want to give up her career and she doesn't want to cost me mine."

"Oh, man! I have been in your shoes. When my wife and I were dating, my business was in Tampa. Rogue lived in Gainesville. So, I sold my business in Tampa and opened Identity Bank in Gainesville."

"That's cool, but I'm not sure I have that degree of flexibility."

Tristan chuckles. "Yeah, my approach had a few downsides. For one, it totally freaked Rogue out. She had a thing about me spending my fortune just to be with her."

"Yeah, I can see how she would feel that way. I'm glad you guys worked it out. Unfortunately, I'm not sure it's going to be that easy for us."

Tristan sits down at one of the tables in the break room and pulls a peanut butter and jelly sandwich out of his lunch bag. It always cracks me up when I see him eating such a simple, wholesome lunch when he could afford to have catering brought in every single day. He gestures for me to take a seat.

I pull my lunch out of the microwave and join him at the table.

"Okay, so the objective of this mission is to try to figure out how to get you and Dakota in the same city, right?

"Well yeah, that would certainly make our marriage stronger — if we ever get that far."

"You said Dakota works out of Arlington, Virginia, correct?"

I nod. "Yeah, that's where Fitzgerald Forensics is

headquartered."

Tristan steeples his fingers under his chin. "You know there is an Elliott's House slated to open in Falls Church, Virginia. I haven't hired a manager yet. I think you would be perfect for the job."

"Me? I don't have experience managing a nonprofit agency like Elliott's House. I'm just a washed up helicopter pilot who works as a bodyguard for you."

"I know. I read your resume and background check when I hired you. I'm always amazed when people assume I don't. I had an almost identical discussion with Jameson Payne before I hired him. That man has been one of my strongest hires. I believe you are uniquely qualified to be a manager at Elliott's House."

"How so?"

"The goal of Elliott's house is to provide resources for families who have lost loved ones. You know what it's like to lose a parent at a young age. You can identify with these families more than most. I value empathy and compassion more than a perfect resume with all the requisite experience. You didn't have any experience as a bodyguard before I hired you. You rose to that challenge with no difficulty. I expect you to perform no less admirably at Elliott's House."

I blow a breath out as I ponder what my boss is offering. "Sir, this is completely overwhelming. Let me think about it first."

Smiling, Tristan says, "Let me put a wrinkle in this for you. That is not your only option. If Dakota would rather change employers, I would love to give her a permanent position on the Cold Case Squadron. She would be a real asset."

"I agree. But I don't know what she would think about moving. Her mom is still in Virginia."

"I understand. So, talk to your girlfriend and figure out which direction you guys want to go. Whatever you decide, I'll make it work."

"Have I mentioned you are the best boss ever?" I announce as I fight back tears.

Tristan grins. "I have heard that a time or two in my life. I believe in building families. It's what makes me tick."

As I leave the weekly staff meeting, I walk by my desk and put the file away. It's funny, before I met Dakota, I would have given anything for a performance evaluation like the one I just received. Now, the diplomat's praise just makes my decision even more difficult. It's a plum assignment, but not if it costs me Dakota. I've made that mistake once and I learned my lesson.

As I am loosening my tie, my cell phone rings in my hand. "Dakota, your ears must be burning. I was just thinking about you."

I hear a low chuckle on the other end of the phone. "Sorry mate, it's only me."

"If you're calling for Dakota, she went out for lunch with her friends. Come to think of it, why are you calling this number?"

"I called you because you are the expert. I'm worried about Dakota."

The hairs on the back of my neck stand up. "Any particular reason why?"

I hear Jamie expel a rough sigh. "I didn't even think about it. We are swamped with work because some crime network featured Fitzgerald Forensics again. So our phones have been ringing off the hook left and right."

"Good for your boss, I guess," I comment.

Although I can't see him, I can almost feel Jamie's shrug. "Most of the time it would be great news. But it means we're using a temp agency to deal with the influx of calls. The gal today was not up to speed on our security protocols. When someone called and pretended to be Dakota's dad, she disclosed Dakota's current location and phone number. I know Dakota doesn't have anything to do with her father. So it must be related to that person following her."

I rub my temple as my head pounds. I take a deep breath and let it out. "Thanks for the heads up, Jamie. Identity Bank has it handled."

We do have a handle on it. But I'm not going to disclose the details to Jamie. I'm not a huge fan of Jamie, even though Dakota seems to have some sort of affection toward him. To me, he comes across as entirely too cocky. In the back of my mind, I wonder if he might be helping Sheldon Harper because Dakota chose me over him.

After a few moments of awkward silence, Jamie clears his throat. "Well, I need to get back to work because we are slammed. I just thought I should let you know what happened."

"Thanks. I appreciate that."

"Hey, Nick, do me a favor and take care of Dakota. She deserves some happiness in her life for a change. I want her to have a great life even if it doesn't involve me."

Something in his tone makes me question my earlier

assumption. Maybe he is just a well-meaning friend. "I'll do my best to keep her safe. Thanks for calling."

After I hang up, I call Tristan. "Nick, I thought you'd be out celebrating. It's not often one of our clients specifically requests a bodyguard."

"Yeah, I was flattered but I think I'd rather stick with the Cold Case Squadron for now. I called about Dakota. One of her coworkers says her father contacted her workplace and was told her exact address and phone number."

Tristan gives a low whistle. "I wondered when it was going to come to this. Fortunately, we've got the jump on him."

"What do you mean?"

"After you reported the license plate of the car that was following you to the movie theater, I had one of our employees place a magnetic tracking device in the wheel well of Sheldon Harper's car."

"You're sure it's him?" I ask.

"Yep," Tristan responds. "He bought it a few months ago after he was paroled."

"Any idea where he is now?"

I hear Tristan rapidly typing on his computer. "It looks like he's at The Oaks Mall. That's odd. I don't know why he would choose that as a target."

"Son of a — !" I exclaim as I take off in a dead sprint toward my car. "Send Cody over for backup! The women are there having lunch. Thank goodness Pauline is with them. Send her a text and give her a heads up. I'm on my way!"

"Ten-four. Don't get yourself killed getting there.

Pauline is more than capable. I've seen Tori spar with Cody and she's no slouch either."

"That only works if they know the threat is incoming."

As I sprint through the doors of the mall, the security guard gives me an alarmed look until he realizes who I am. I've worked with Tristan on several security system installations. I motion for him to follow me. Fortunately, Dakota and I have been to this restaurant many times and I know exactly where it's located. My heart pounds as I jog through the mall with the security guard trailing me. My heart about just about stops when I charge around the corner.

Sheldon Harper has a gun trained on Dakota's temple. In turn, Pauline has her service revolver pointed at him. Pauline sees me out of the corner of her eye. "I hope you brought backup, Weston. I could use a hand here."

Dakota gasps when she opens her eyes and finds me a few feet in front of her. "He's crazy, Nick! Don't get hurt!"

"Cavalry should be here any minute," I answer through clenched teeth. Louder, I say, "Sheldon Harper, you have no business here. Leave Dakota alone! Haven't you done enough damage in her life?"

Dakota's father recklessly swings his revolver around and points it in my general direction. "This is none of your business!" he screams. "If this mongrel had the decency to die the first time, I would not have had to do this. She ruined my life! I could've gotten away with everything if she hadn't testified against me! I promised her I would be back and I'm just keeping my word."

"For the first time ever," Dakota murmurs bitterly.

"Do you hear that disrespect? That's why she needs to just die once and for all."

"You want a fight with somebody? How about choosing somebody your own size," I taunt.

In a moment reminiscent of every nightmare I've ever had, the older man comes charging at me like a high school wrestler. In that moment, I hear a loud bang and smell gun smoke. Before my eyes, he crumples to the ground. Startled, I look around and find Pauline holstering her weapon. She nods at the security guard. "Call 911 and ask for medical and Captain Schumaker. Obviously there's been an officer involved shooting." Pauline leans down and cuffs Sheldon Harper's wrist to a nearby table before she attempts to clear his airway.

In that instant, my military training kicks in and I start to perform CPR. I pause for a moment while Pauline checks for a pulse. After a minute or so, Pauline shakes her head sadly. "You can continue until rescue gets here, but I don't think it'll do much good. Crap! I wanted to stop him but I didn't really want to kill him."

Tori leans down and pats Pauline on the shoulder. "It was a justified shooting. No one is going to argue any different. Dakota and Nick were both in grave danger."

The security guard nods. "That was a righteous takedown." He points up toward the ceiling. "We got it all on video if anybody's got any questions. I'm just glad you were here so no one else got hurt."

When Pauline stands up, I can see her hands shaking. "Still, it's not the way I wanted it to end. Captain Schumaker is going to have kittens."

Dakota runs over and gives Pauline a hug. "I owe you

my life. My dad tried to kill me once and he wouldn't have stopped until he was dead. Thank you for giving me my life back."

Dakota lets out a sob before she runs into my arms. "I can't thank you enough. You made it possible for Pauline to save me. I knew the risk was out there, I just didn't realize how horrifying it would be to come face-to-face with the man who almost murdered me."

I take a deep breath and let it out slowly as I try to control my heartrate. That was as close to death as I've been since I was shot down. I gather her close and kiss her tenderly. "I love you and I will always have your back."

As I wipe tears from her eyes with the pads of my thumbs, she whispers, "I can never thank you enough for being my hero." She looks down at the crumpled body on the floor. "Before you, I never thought men like you existed."

# EPILOGUE

# DAKOTA

On a crisp March day in Tennessee, we are waiting to be cleared by security so we can enter the courtroom. Ever chivalrous, Nick places his jacket around my shoulders and warms my hands in his. I glance behind me to see the growing lineup. As I study people to see who might be supporting Shalonda, I am shocked to see a woman who looks like my mom.

"Mom! What are you doing here?" I ask, my voice sharper than I intend because of my utter shock.

My mom rushes toward me and stands next to me. "There you are! Nick told me you might need me for moral support today. I can't believe he flew me all the way from Virginia to Tennessee so I could see this."

I look back and forth between my mother and Nick like I'm watching a tennis match. "Wait... You've been talking to Nick?"

My mom looks sheepish. "After Nick saved you from your father, I started thinking about all the things I don't know about him. So ... you know Bob Patton, the detective who helped us after the house fire?"

I raise an eyebrow. "What about Detective Patton?" My stomach is in a tight knot.

My mom rushes to explain, "Well, he's retired now. So I asked him to look into your boyfriend. I have to say, Detective Patton was very impressed. He says your boyfriend has a stellar military record and is highly recommended by his boss. I'm so sorry for jumping to conclusions. I just didn't want you to end up with anyone like your father. That was an absolute nightmare."

Nick steps forward and sticks out his hand for her to shake. "Hello, it's nice to see you again. Ma'am, I would've been happy to share my criminal background check with you. All you had to do was ask. I want nothing but the best for your daughter. I love her with all my heart."

My mom fans herself with her hand. "Oh my, you are such a gentleman. Just like Bob told me you would be. I'm sorry I prejudged you. Dakota looks so happy. I was watching you all take care of each other. It's a beautiful thing. Nick was telling me about your new job at Identity Bank. I'm so proud of you, but I'm going to miss you —"

Our conversation stops briefly as we go through the security line. It's a little awkward when Nick has to take off his belt. But, he handled it with good humor. I guess I'm lucky I didn't have to remove my earrings.

As happy as I am to see my mom making peace with Nick, my nerves are starting to get the best of me. After my mom makes it through security, I comment, "I can't believe you came all the way for this court proceeding. I don't think I'll even be testifying. It's my understanding the defendant is entering an Alford plea."

"What's that?" my mom asks.

"It's a legal maneuver which allows a defendant to

admit that the state has enough evidence to convict them without actually having to say they are guilty."

My mom gasps. "Oh, how terrible for your family. I know what it's like to not be able to confront my abuser in court. It's an awful feeling."

Nick grimaces. "Yeah, my family isn't too happy about it because it takes the death penalty off the table. So, if she had gone through trial, the jury might have found her guilty on the most serious charges. I don't understand why the state accepted the deal. It seems pretty cut and dry. She confessed to killing my niece. I have my own feelings about what should happen to people like her."

I put my hand on Nick's arm. "I know it's hard to understand. What Shalonda did was the definition of evil, but in the eyes of the law, she had no prior convictions and a jury might feel sympathetic about the circumstances. After all, Shalonda comes across as mentally fragile. I suspect the District Attorney's Office didn't want to take any chances. Some jail time is better than an acquittal."

Nick growls. "The DA said stuff along those lines, and I guess I have to trust them, but I don't have to like it."

A pair of bailiffs open the court room doors for us. There something about the majestic wood paneling in the room that reminds me of the church I used to attend when I was younger. It feels very somber and claustrophobic in here. I'm second guessing my decision to be here.

Nick laces his fingers through mine as we walk toward the front of the courtroom. "We've got this. It'll only last a few minutes."

"I know. I should be happy we caught the killer, but I just feel sad. Obviously your sister-in-law wasn't in her right mind. Even if she is punished, it won't bring Harmony

Hope back."

"Where should we sit?" Nick whispers.

When I see Cheryl sitting alone, my heart breaks. I can't imagine what she must be feeling in this moment. I put my hand on Nick's shoulder. "Let's sit here beside Cheryl."

Nick looks puzzled by my suggestion but shrugs. He tries to step aside to allow me to into the aisle first, but I stop him. "You guys have been friends since childhood, she'll need your support right now," I whisper.

After he sits down, Cheryl catches my eye and mouths the word, "Thank you."

I mouth back, "Any time."

When Milo and Thea come in a few minutes later, they sit beside my mother. After what seems like an eternity, the bailiff calls the courtroom to order. We all stand and I notice Cheryl is a bit shaky. Instinctively, Nick puts his arm around her waist to steady her. I have to remind myself that Nick is just being kind and whatever was between him and Cheryl is long over.

The bailiff announces the case number and the judge approaches the bench. She gavels court into session. After we've all sat down, she addresses Shalonda's attorney. "Is the defendant ready to enter a plea?"

"We are, Your Honor. Shalonda Weston Jones wishes to enter an Alford plea as it pertains to the death of Harmony Hope Scroggins."

"Ms. Jones, do you understand the ramifications of this choice? Although this is not a guilty plea, you are essentially agreeing that the state has enough evidence to find you guilty of murder if the case was to go to trial," the judge instructs.

Shalonda leans into the microphone and mumbles, "Yes, Your Honor."

"Before I invoke your sentence, the people you hurt have something to say to you. Please do not interrupt their victim impact statements. Bailiff, please escort the first witness to the stand."

On shaky legs, Cheryl stands up. "I need to do this before I lose my nerve," she murmurs under her breath.

She sits down in the witness chair and leans into the microphone as she addresses Shalonda. "You and I had the misfortune of falling for the same guy. I'll admit, I was wrong to encourage him to cheat on you. You could've done lots of things like blast me on Facebook or badmouth me around town. I deserved all of that, but you did not have a reason to kill an innocent child for my mistake. I cannot imagine what Harmony's last moments were like. I don't even want to because if I did, I would want to die too. You destroyed my life because you didn't approve of my choices. I hope you pay the price for your choice to kill my only child." Cheryl openly sobs. She looks up at the judge. "I am so sorry, I can't do this anymore. I don't want to see her for the rest of my life. If I had my way, she would get the death penalty just like my daughter."

The judge nods. "Thank you for sharing. Does anyone else have a statement?"

Slowly, Milo rises to his feet. "I do, Your Honor."

The judge gestures toward the witness stand. "You may proceed."

Milo sits down and wipes away a tear before addressing his former wife. "I don't even know what to say. I've been thinking about this for two years and I still don't have any answers. Shalonda, you once were my everything. Like

Cheryl, I wish I hadn't made such a terrible mistake. But, I not only lost my daughter — one I didn't even know I had — I lost my love for you. I don't even know how to put into words how much you've cost me. I will never see my daughter start first grade, get her driver's license or get married. You not only killed her, you killed the future that could have been. I'll never understand how someone who professed to love children so much could do something so evil and demented to a little baby. Because I've loved you for most of my adult life, I struggle with what your punishment should be. On one hand, you murdered an innocent child. On the other, the Shalonda I know couldn't hurt anyone. So, I'm stuck between the woman I loved and the real woman who smothered a child who was too small to fight back." He looks up at the judge. "I'm glad I'm not in charge of deciding your fate, but I hope the sentence you receive provides payback for what you did to my daughter." With that, Milo abruptly stands up and leaves the stand. I can see his chest heaving as he attempts to control his emotions. Nick stands up and hugs his brother as Milo takes a seat. My eyes widen in surprise as I watch Nick make his way up to the witness stand.

"I'm here on behalf of Harmony Hope's extended family. I may only be her uncle but we have been harmed too. Initially, I was considered a murder suspect. Such an accusation could have destroyed my career. My mother was completely devasted by the loss of a grandchild she never got to meet. I know you had a vendetta against Cheryl and my brother. I'm not happy about their relationship either, but that's no justification to kill a child. I hope the judge in this case understands how you've changed who our family is. In my eyes, there isn't a punishment severe enough for you, but I will have to accept whatever the court deems is proper. Just remember, what you put out into the world, you get back. I hope you get it back tenfold." Nick flicks tears out of his eyes before he stands up and leaves the stand.

"Anyone else?" The judge asks as she surveys the courtroom. "Very well then, thank you all for your powerful testimonies. I wish I could do more, but per the terms of this Alford plea agreement, you are hereby sentenced to thirty to forty-five years in the state penitentiary. I understand you have expressed no remorse. I am not the final arbiter. May God have mercy on your soul." With that, the judge hits the bench with the gavel and leaves the courtroom.

My mom gasps before she announces, "Thirty years isn't long enough for someone who killed an innocent baby. I know what that feels like. Thank heavens, Sheldon Harper is dead now. Is it wrong of me to wish Shalonda was dead too? "

"Mom, I understand your pain. But, at least Shalonda is off the streets and unable to hurt anyone else and maybe that's all we can expect from the justice system."

Cheryl leans forward so she can see past Nick and me. "It's not justice for Harmony Hope. I'll have a life sentence of guilt and pain while she has a chance to get out of jail — none of this is fair!"

Just then, the bailiffs start to escort Shalonda out of the courtroom. As she turns, she catches sight of us. "Why aren't you arresting them?" Shalonda shouts across the courtroom "They're the ones who made me do this."

Nick stands up abruptly. "No, Shalonda! That's not how it went and you know it. No one was involved in this crime except you. My brother and Cheryl are not responsible for your reaction even if you were hurt. Don't put this on them!"

Nick sits down as quickly as he stood up. We glare at his sister-in-law until we can no longer see her. "I can't believe how selfish she turned out to be," he comments under his breath.

Milo looks at him and says, "Me either, brother. Me either. I can only hope she's treated in prison about as well as she treated my daughter."

My mother murmurs, "Amen to that."

We make a very unlikely lunch group as we all go to a local diner. Cheryl and Milo are quietly talking while my mother is not so subtly playing twenty questions with Nick.

After dinner, Cheryl taps her milkshake glass with the tip of her knife. "I have something to say. I know this may seem odd, but I want to thank Dakota for letting me know what happened to my daughter. I never dreamed the outcome would be this horrible, but at least now I know what happened to her. I am in a much better place now than I was back then. Although Bubba couldn't be here today, he wanted me to thank the Weston family for their support during this terrible tragedy."

She clears her throat before she continues. "Milo, I'm sorry the person you love robbed you of what you wanted most in the world. There won't ever be a day that I don't feel guilty about my decisions."

Shyly, she pivots toward Thea. "You raised some fine young men, Mrs. Weston. I'm sorry our actions hurt everyone involved; that was never my intent. Honestly, I fell a little bit in love with both of your sons."

Thea examines Cheryl as she would a bug. "I can't say I'll ever understand why you made the choices you did. I'm sorry you had to pay this kind of price for your mistakes. If the boys can forgive you, so can I," she adds.

"Thank you so much Mrs. Weston. That means a lot to me."

Cheryl turns to me. "Dakota, I want you to know Nick is a great man. I didn't realize how amazing he was until after it was far too late. I'm sorry my actions brought heartache into your lives, but I'm grateful that you love Nick. For many years, Nick was my very best friend. I want only amazing things to happen to him. I think you are one of those amazing things. Thank you so much for helping to bring peace to my friends and family."

My cheeks heat and I'm sure they are bright red. "I'm not sure I deserve all the credit for bringing this amazing family together. You are all each other's strengths. I set out to find justice for a little girl without a name. You could have sent me away and not helped me solve the mystery of Harmony Hope — yet you stuck by me even when you were annoyed by the information I presented. Not only that, Nick saved me and my family from a man completely dedicated to destroying our lives."

Nick places his arm around my shoulders. "It was the least I could do. I love you with my whole heart and I would be devastated if anything happened to you."

I wipe away tears. "I feel the same way about you. I am a better person because you love me." I address the rest of the people sitting at the table, "You all are the true heroes. I want you all to know that because of my experience with you, Milo, Nick and Thea, I'll be devoting my career to helping find missing children who have gotten lost in the cracks so we can provide more families with a measure of justice."

Thea walks over to me and gives me a big hug. "Honestly, I was righteously mad at you when we first met, but now I understand you were just trying to find a lost little girl. I don't know if you realize this, you also rescued a lost little boy. Nick isn't so young anymore, but he'll always be my baby boy. It's obvious he is over the moon happy with you. Thank you for helping my boy find hope again."

With a flourish, Nick pulls a black velvet box out of his pocket. This time, I am prepared for the beautiful diamond and sapphire ring. "I've waited as long as I possibly could for this mess to be over. I never thought it would take two years for it to come to trial. But you're officially done with my family, right — no more investigation?"

Mutely, I nod as I fight back tears of joy.

"I'm going to ask again, Dakota Hope Crenshaw, will you marry me? There is nothing between us but love now and I don't ever want to let you go."

I pull Nick to a standing position and launch myself into his arms. I start dropping kisses all over his face. "This time the answer is yes with absolutely no equivocation. I love you." My hands are trembling as Nick slides my engagement ring on my finger.

Without warning, tears begin to flow from my eyes as all my stress melts away. Nick reaches into his jacket pocket and pulls out a tissue. As he hands it to me, he whispers, "Yep, you're going to need a wedding dress with pockets for sure."

"You are a good man, Nick Weston. You changed my life in all the best ways. When I first met you, I felt ugly and broken. You told me once that you wished I could see myself the way you do. I'm starting to see the vision and it looks beautiful. I can't wait until we get married — even if there are a few tears involved."

Dear Reader,

Thanks for giving my book a read. If you liked reading about people who are not so stereotypical, then I've got good news…

…there's more.

If you missed it the first time, now is your chance to pick up Love and Injustice. Love and Injustice is Cody Erickson's story and is more of a suspenseful/police procedural romance than some of my earlier stuff. So, I recently re-released a new edition of this book and started a new series called Hidden Hearts — Protection Unit. I think you'll love this workplace romance with a strong heroine and friends to lovers themes.

What if her innocence doesn't matter?

Tori Clarkson has spent her life fighting for justice as a prosecutor.

Now, she can't even save her own career.

Detective Cody Erickson needs her help to save some

missing kids.

She is powerless to help him this time.

Will he understand, or will he assume she is guilty like everyone else?

Can true love overcome injustice?

!~Mary

Because love matters, differences don't.

# ACKNOWLEDGEMENTS

First and foremost, I want to acknowledge my behind-the-scenes expert on all of my books, Kathern Watts. She has done a phenomenal job of critiquing my words to make them stronger. I am so grateful for your presence in my life.

Secondly, I would like to thank my number one fan and research partner, Kathy Faltinson. You give me the oddest bits of helpful information at just the right time.

Lisa Lee is my amazing editor. Although there are often many things to correct, Lisa's feedback is always affirming and spot on. Thank for making me a better author.

Lacie Redding, my fellow night owl and personal assistant extraordinaire. Thank you for helping readers get excited about what I do. I couldn't do this without your help.

~*~

In the time since I last released a book, my husband and best friend battled cancer. He is still in the process of recovering. However, even when he hurts, Leonard takes amazing care of me and makes it possible for me to devote my time to writing.

My youngest son, Justin earned his driver's license. Thank you for being my chauffeur and keeping me well-stocked with McDonald's unsweet tea.

# Finding Hope

My oldest son, Brandon, is a doctor. Although his specialty is currently family medicine, he has been serving on the front lines in this pandemic. I would appreciate it if you could keep him in your thoughts and prayers.


For all the fans who stand by me when my production schedule is interrupted by one health crisis or another, I can't thank you enough for your support. Thank you so much for believing that because love matters, differences don't.

# ABOUT THE AUTHOR

I have been lucky enough to live my own version of a romance novel. I married the guy who kissed me at summer camp. He told me on the night we met that he was going to marry me and be the father of my children.

Eventually, I stopped giggling when he said it, and we've been married for more than thirty years. We have two children. The oldest is a Doctor of Osteopathy. He is across the United States completing his residency, but when he's done, he is going to come back to Oregon and practice Family Medicine. Our youngest son is now tackling high school, where he is an honor student. He hasn't quite decided what career he wants to pursue in the future, but I'm sure he will be brilliant at whatever he endeavors to do.

I write full time now. I have published more than three dozen books and have several more underway. I volunteer my time to a variety of causes. I have worked as a Civil Rights Attorney and diversity advocate. I spent several years working for various social service agencies before becoming an attorney.

In my spare time, I love to cook, decorate cakes and, of course, I obsessively, compulsively read.

I would be honored if you would take a few moments out of your busy day to check out my website, MaryCrawfordAuthor.com. While you're there, you can sign up for my newsletter and get a free book. I will be announcing my upcoming books and giving sneak peeks as well as sponsoring giveaways and giving you information about other interesting events.

If you have questions or comments, please E-mail me at Mary@MaryCrawfordAuthor.com or find me on the following social networks:

Facebook: www.facebook.com/authormarycrawford

Website: MaryCrawfordAuthor.com

Twitter: www.twitter.com/MaryCrawfordAut